4th g

DAUGHTERS

of the DESERT

Stories of Remarkable Women
from Christian,
Jewish,
and Muslim
Traditions

CLAIRE RUDOLF MURPHY

MEGHAN NUTTALL SAYRES

MARY CRONK FARRELL

SARAH CONOVER

BETSY WHARTON

Walking Together, Finding the Way
SKYLIGHT PATHS Publishing
Woodstock, Vermont

Daughters of the Desert:
Stories of Remarkable Women from Christian, Jewish, and Muslim Traditions

2005 First Quality Paperback Edition
2003 Second Hardcover Printing
2003 First Hardcover Printing
© 2003 by Claire Rudolf Murphy, Meghan Nuttall Sayres,
Mary Cronk Farrell, Sarah Conover, and Betsy Wharton

Cover illustration © 2003 by SkyLight Paths Publishing

All rights reserved. No part of this book may be reproduced or transmitted in any form or by any means, electronic or mechanical, including photocopying, recording, or by any information storage and retrieval system, without permission in writing from the publisher.

For information regarding permission to reprint material from this book, please mail or fax your request in writing to SkyLight Paths Publishing, Permissions Department, at the address/fax number listed below.

Library of Congress Cataloging-in-Publication Data
Daughters of the desert : stories of remarkable women from Christian, Jewish, and Muslim traditions / Claire Rudolf Murphy ... [et al.].
    p. cm.
Includes bibliographical references.
ISBN 1-893361-72-1 (hc.)
1. Women in the Bible—Biography. 2. Bible—Biography. 3. Women in the Koran—Biography. 4. Koran—Biography. I. Murphy, Claire Rudolf.
BS575.D343 2003
220.9'2'082—dc21   2002153821

ISBN 1-59473-106-3 (pbk.)

10   9   8   7   6   5   4   3   2   1
Manufactured in the United States

Art by Sara Dismukes
Cover Design by Stacey Hood

> SkyLight Paths Publishing is creating a place where people of different spiritual traditions come together for challenge and inspiration, a place where we can help each other understand the mystery that lies at the heart of our existence.
>
> SkyLight Paths sees both believers and seekers as a community that increasingly transcends traditional boundaries of religion and denomination—people wanting to learn from each other, *walking together, finding the way.*

SkyLight Paths, "Walking Together, Finding the Way," and colophon are trademarks of LongHill Partners, Inc., registered in the U.S. Patent and Trademark Office.

Walking Together, Finding the Way
Published by SkyLight Paths Publishing
A Division of LongHill Partners, Inc.
Sunset Farm Offices, Rte. 4, P.O. Box 237
Woodstock, VT 05091
Tel: (802) 457-4000   Fax: (802) 457-4004
www.skylightpaths.com

Best wishes,

For our daughters

בנות המדבר

ὑπὲρ τῶν θυγατέρων ἡμῶν

إهداء إلى بناتنا

Claire
Rudolf

CONTENTS

CHRISTIAN STORIES

MUSLIM STORIES

TIMELINE OF THE STORIES*

Eve ————————	Time of biblical creation
Hebrew calendar begins ————	3,762 B.C.E. (Before Common Era)
Hagar ———————— Abraham *Sarah*	1850–2000
Shiphrah ——————— Moses *Miriam*	1200–1300
Huldah ———————	625
Esther ————————	538
Shoshana ———————	300
Mary of Nazareth ———— Jesus is born Christian calendar begins	Common Era begins
Eleni ———————— *Salome* *Binah* *Mary Magdalene*	30–40 C.E.
Lydia ————————	50
Muhammad is born ————	570
Khadija ——————— Hijrah, migration from Mecca to Medina – Muslim calendar begins	610 622
Fatima ——————— *Zarah* *Aisha*	625 630 656

* These dates are only intended to be approximations.

INTRODUCTION

*D*aughters of the Desert tells the stories of eighteen
women of the ancient world who lived in the same
desert homeland, some 4,000 to 1,300 years ago. Many
of them were descendants of the patriarch Abraham.
Instead of worshiping many gods, they were among the
first to worship one God. Their stories celebrate the similarities and differences among the Christian, Jewish, and
Muslim traditions that enrich our lives even today.

Although women played key roles in all three
religions from the very beginning, their stories were
seldom recorded. Women in the ancient world rarely
had the opportunity to learn to read and write. The
men who recorded and copied the sacred Scriptures
and other sacred texts included very little about how
mothers passed on their experiences of God through
storytelling, song, and ritual.

To discover more about these remarkable women,
we used our imaginations and careful research to explore
between the lines of each religion's sacred writings.
Although these stories took place long ago, you may recognize some of the same hopes and struggles that people
experience today. We hope you will enjoy meeting these
women and will come to know them as we have.

JEWISH STORIES

A THOUSAND WRINKLES

The child grew up and was weaned, and Abraham held a great feast on the day Isaac was weaned.
—Hebrew Bible, Genesis 21:8

Sarah added the last ingredients to the syrupy compote: dates, almonds, figs, and the luscious oranges that she had bought from a trader in Kadesh. She couldn't wait to see her young son's face when he tasted this special treat. That morning, for the first time, Isaac had gone with his half-brother, Ishmael, to lead the sheep down from the high pasture. Now that Isaac was weaned, he would spend his days working with the older boys; no longer would she have him by her side. The long-awaited feast would begin as soon as they returned.

"Shalom, Sarah!" She heard the booming voice of King Abimelech, who had just arrived with his family. She dried her hands and went out to greet her guests.

"Welcome to all of you!" she called. "You must be exhausted after your long journey." Sarah smiled at the old chieftain and his wife, Amidta. As she did so, the weariness instantly left their faces, and the dust that covered their robes seemed to vanish.

"Our hardship is already forgotten," the old man chuckled.

"Welcome, Abimelech! May peace be with you." Sarah's husband, Abraham, stepped up and clasped his old friend on the shoulder.

"And peace be with you as well, my friend," replied Abimelech. He looked up toward the sky where a billowy white cloud, etched in gold, hung like a canopy over their heads. "I see that your invisible God continues to bless your house."

While the old friends talked, Sarah looked toward the ravine north of the tents. Despite her white hair and weathered face, her hearing was keen. She listened intently, sorting out the various sounds: the voices of guests, the music of a lyre and a drum. "Abraham, I think I hear the boys down in the ravine," she said.

"Nonsense, Sarah. Our sons would not wander down there."

"Yes, it is strange," she replied. "But I can hear them. I'll go and fetch them." Hurrying off to find the boys, Sarah left the guests still talking near the tents.

Sarah reached the edge of the ravine and peered down through the palms and grasses that lined the narrow canyon. She could not see the boys, but she could recognize their quarreling voices. She was unable to make out any of the words that were spoken, but the scene had a familiar ring.

Sarah sped down the steep slope, climbing over boulders and pushing her way through the brush to reach the bottom of the ravine.

"Ishmael, what are you doing in the ravine? Isaac is too small to come in here."

"We were looking for turtles," Ishmael quickly offered.

"Ishmael pushed me down on the rocks," Isaac whimpered.

"It was an accident, Isaac. I was just trying to help you climb out of the stream bed."

"No, it wasn't an accident—"

Sarah broke in. "Why must you boys quarrel on this festive day?"

"There's no reason for *me* to celebrate," Ishmael replied. "Today I'm being replaced at the table by this baby who can't even tie his own shirt."

"I am not a baby!" Isaac cried out to his older half-brother.

"Isaac, come with me." Sarah took him by the hand. "The guests are waiting for you. Ishmael will join us at the feast when he's ready."

As they climbed up the steep trail, Sarah asked Isaac about his first day out with the flock. Isaac, who ordinarily bubbled with chatter and laughter, did not answer any of his mother's questions. He walked silently all the way back to camp.

During the feast, Sarah had no appetite, no heart for celebration. She excused herself early and found a quiet corner of the tent, where she sat watching Abraham with his two sons: Isaac on his right, sitting on Abraham's knee; and Ishmael on his left, nearly a grown man. The older boy entertained the men with tales about his hunting adventures, for Ishmael was already a skilled bowman. Isaac listened and laughed along with the rest. Both boys seemed unconcerned about the afternoon's quarrel. Nonetheless, Sarah could not shake her troubled feelings.

She thought back to Ishmael's birth. Childless for all those years, she had arranged for her maidservant Hagar to conceive in her place. It had been such a joyous time when Ishmael was born. Who could have imagined that fourteen years later she would miraculously give birth to her own child? Isaac's birth had surprised everyone. But for Ishmael, who was the son of a maidservant, it meant the loss of his inheritance.

Night fell and the lanterns were lit. There would be singing and storytelling until daylight as the celebration continued. Isaac had fallen asleep beside the fire.

Sarah lifted him up and carried him to bed in her tent. She watched Isaac's delicate breath as he slept. Isaac had grown into a fine lad and yet he was still young and vulnerable.

She arose and walked out into the clear night. The stars were thick in the heavens. Her mind raced ahead of her feet. So much turmoil in the family—she thought about Ishmael. Sarah had loved him as if he had been her own son. But Isaac was her flesh, her darling. As the heir, Isaac, her son, would inherit despite his youth, and Ishmael would not.

Sarah had tried everything she knew to make peace within the family, but jealousy and resentment still smoldered around them all. *What more can I do to make peace in this family? Adonai, help me to see.*

God did not speak to Sarah in dreams or visions, but she had learned to listen to the quiet insights that came like whispers on the air. She saw a raven take flight. Stroking wings lifted the bird high into the cloudless night. She watched as the bird flew into the distance, disappearing into the starry heavens. Sarah listened to the wind for a long time, until finally she knew what she had to do.

Sarah walked to Abraham's tent and entered. "Husband, rouse yourself. I have something urgent to tell you."

"What is it, Sarah?" Abraham pulled himself out of sleep. "What can be so urgent that it cannot wait until morning?"

"The rivalry between your two sons is worsening. It is best for everyone if we separate them." Then she told him the story of their quarreling in the ravine.

"It is only a simple boyhood rivalry," Abraham answered. "They are fine boys, both favored by God. They will outgrow their struggle."

"No, they will *not* outgrow this," she said. Then, drawing in a deep breath, she continued. "Remember how it has gone with Ishmael. As your firstborn, he spent fourteen years of his boyhood believing that he would receive your inheritance. Then Isaac's birth changed everything for him. Who would have believed that you and I could conceive a child, old as we were? Yet the Lord gave us this miracle child to fulfill the Covenant. Adonai promised to bless Ishmael, but he cannot share in the Covenant with Isaac. Listen to me, Abraham, there will not be peace between these brothers as long as they remain together in this house. One will torment the other, and so in exchange."

"And what do you suggest I do about it, Sarah?"

"I have struggled for months to find a way toward peace for our family. And tonight at the edge of the ravine, I became certain. You must cast out the slave woman and her son together. Ishmael is a fine marksman; they will make their way. It is best for them to go immediately."

Abraham eased his ancient frame so that he could rest on a goatskin cushion. "Sarah, you have always been jealous of Hagar. Is that the true source of your request?"

Caught off guard by this question, Sarah paused to consider her answer. "It is true that I have envied Hagar over the years. But I am old now, and the flame of my jealousy has gone out. It is cool like morning ash. Ishmael must depart with his mother, of this I am certain."

"I will consider this matter," Abraham said, his voice somber. "But Ishmael is my son, and he will always have a place in my house."

Sarah laid her hand on her aged husband's shoulder. She held his gaze in hers and then went out into the night.

The next morning, Sarah stood atop a small hillock beside her tent, watching the dawn light spread pink across the sky. On most days sunrise was her favorite time—that cool moment before the sun dries the dew and the air is spiced with the tangy scent of the tamarisk. Sarah saw Abraham walk toward Hagar's tent. She heard voices; there was a great wailing. They were pleading. Abraham gave Hagar and Ishmael a goatskin of water and a bag of provisions. He walked with them to the edge of the camp, and then he embraced each one, first the mother and then the son. And then Hagar and Ishmael set out into the expanse of morning.

Sarah tried to hold back tears. She clenched her jaw to keep from calling out to them, to stop the leaving.

After they had disappeared into the horizon, Abraham came to join his wife on the hillock. He laid his hand on her shoulder. Abraham's tender touch melted her resolve. Sarah's face collapsed into a thousand wrinkles, and she wept.

Seeing that his wife's grief matched his own, Abraham said, "Adonai has assured me that this is the right action. They will be blessed. Their descendants will be a great nation."

"And may Adonai," Sarah said, "lead us all toward peace."

ABOUT THE STORY

Of the many episodes of Sarah's life that appear in the book of Genesis (chapters 12–24), this story best illustrates the common roots shared by the Jewish, Christian, and Muslim traditions. Sarah's descendants through Isaac gave rise to the Jewish people, and Hagar's descendants through Ishmael gave rise to the Arab people and thus to Islam. "A Thousand

Wrinkles" deals with a conflict within Abraham's family that resulted in the first branching of the family tree.

There are many ways to interpret Sarah's role in this story. No doubt she felt jealousy and a protective instinct toward her son. But her deep faith in God's Covenant and her compassionate desire to promote peace also motivated Sarah. She saw a painful conflict within her family and was courageous enough to take action.

A similar story in this book, "The Waters of Zamzam," presents the Muslim version of Hagar and Ishmael's sojourn in the desert. As you compare the stories, you will see some important differences between the two.

B. W.

RIVER JOURNEY

Then the king of Egypt spoke to the Hebrew midwives, one of whom was named Shiphrah, and the other Puah, saying, "When you deliver the Hebrew women, look at the birth stool; if it is a boy, kill him, and if it is a girl, let her live."
—*Hebrew Bible, Exodus 1:15–16*

A soldier's chariot sped through the city, sending up a great cloud of dust in its wake. Inside the chariot, Shiphrah and Puah whispered in hushed tones.

"In the name of Isis, where are they taking us?"

"We have done no wrong," Shiphrah reassured her friend. "We are midwives, loyal to Pharaoh. We have nothing to fear."

With a sudden lurch, they came to a halt. Soldiers pulled the women roughly out of the chariot, into a vast courtyard. "Pharaoh's palace!" Puah exclaimed. "What do they want with us?"

The women stood before a great set of doors inscribed with hieroglyphics and inlaid with brilliant gems. The doors slowly opened to reveal a dazzling

golden chamber, such as Shiphrah had never before imagined. The soldiers motioned for the women to enter.

No sooner had they stepped inside the magnificent room than a soldier shouted at them. "Bow down
before Pharaoh! Death to anyone fool enough to look
upon the face of the God-King!"

The women collapsed to the ground. Shiphrah lay
with her cheek pressed against the marble floor, her
rapid breath like mist on the cool tiles. She could see
nothing from this position except the sandaled feet of
the soldiers as they marched past her in unison. A great
horn was sounded; then a booming voice announced
that Pharaoh would now speak.

"As you well know, it is a time of great suffering
in Egypt. The gods have been made angry, and so they
have withheld the rain and diminished the river Nile.
Drought has overtaken our land and famine has spread."

If only she could see this pharaoh, who spoke the
will of the gods.

"And who is to blame for this misery?" He continued. "I tell you it is the Hebrews. These slaves have
been ordered to work on the building of a great tem
ple, a glorious tribute to Osiris, the great god, ruler of
the underworld. But the Hebrews are arrogant. They
claim allegiance to their desert god, their invisible Yah,
who they say condemns the building of the temple.

Their disobedience has brought hunger to all of Egypt. They must be punished!"

Shiphrah had heard the talk in the marketplace. The work masters had lost control of the laborers. Work on the temple had all but stopped. *But what does this have to do with us?* she wondered. And then as if in answer to her question, she heard Pharaoh say, "And when you assist the Hebrew women as they give birth, if it is a son, you shall kill him. And if it is a daughter, she shall live."

As soon as Pharaoh finished speaking, he left the chamber, and the midwives were released from the palace. Shiphrah and Puah walked home together.

"We deliver life, not death," Puah lamented. "Killing should be a soldier's job. The sword would strike swift fear into their hearts. But what can we do? How can we satisfy the gods—one infant at a time?"

"It is not for us to question Pharaoh's wisdom," Shiphrah replied. "We must do as we have been commanded. We shall certainly be rewarded for our obedience." Shiphrah paused to cast a glance over her shoulder. "Or we shall be punished for our defiance."

Late that night, after serving her family a meager meal of bread and dates, Shiphrah sat alone on her rooftop, unable to sleep. A crescent moon rose above the eastern edge of the city, illuminating the partially built walls of the great temple. Just to the south of the temple, a smoky haze hovered over the low outline of the Hebrew work camp. *Ah, these accursed Hebrews! First their arrogance has caused the gnawing hunger in my belly, and now their punishment is stealing my sleep.*

An excited call from the street below interrupted Shiphrah's thoughts. "Blessings on this house!" She could barely make out the words, spoken as they were in a thick accent. "I seek Shiphrah the midwife!"

Shiphrah hurried down the brick stairs and pulled back the brightly colored tapestry that hung across her doorway. "*Shh,* others are sleeping!"

"My wife," said the man. His bearded face was sharply angled and burned from the sun, his hands callused and rough. "She needs help with the baby."

The man was a Hebrew. Shiphrah flushed and reached for the wall to steady herself. She wasn't ready, not tonight.

"I'm sorry——" she began.

From a small leather pouch, the man unwrapped four brown eggs. "Please. I can pay you."

It had been months since her family had eaten eggs. She thought of her own children, their faces gaunt for lack of meat. Hurriedly, she reached for the eggs. "I'll gather my things."

In the darkened house she crossed the room and lifted a painted figure from a small altar: Taweret, guardian of birth, with the head of a crocodile, paws of a lion, and

15

body of a pregnant hippopotamus. She fingered the smooth curves, the cool weight of the stone. "Grant me this request, gentle Goddess," she whispered to the figure, "may this baby delivered tonight be a girl." She nestled the figure into her leather satchel and went out.

Shiphrah struggled to keep pace with the man as they wound their way through the darkened city. Open squares gave way to narrow lanes and finally to a rough dirt track that led them out of the city. As they entered the Hebrew encampment, the air thickened. The residue of the day's heat and smoke mingled with the smell of animal waste and sweat. Shiphrah lifted her cloak to cover her mouth and nose. The place was crowded with makeshift huts—tents, really. Four walls made of reeds were covered with a bit of drab cloth draped across the top for a roof. Night sounds passed freely through the encampment: a baby crying, a low snoring, the racking cough of dust-choked lungs.

Pharaoh's words echoed in her mind. *If it is a boy, kill him.* She would obey Pharaoh's command, for the good of Egypt. *If it is a boy, kill him.* But how would she do it? She forced her mind to imagine. She would cradle the baby in her arms; then she would turn away, cupping her hand over the mouth and nose, and she would smother it, keeping the baby silent until it gave up its life to her. *But how long, how long will it take before the baby grows still?*

The man stopped and motioned for Shiphrah to enter through a low door. In the gloom, she could see the laboring woman lying on her side, with nothing but a coarse blanket between her and the dirt floor. Her breathing was rapid and her face tense with the effort and the pain. Shiphrah knelt beside her.

"Thank you for coming," gasped the woman. Shiphrah began to prepare a poultice of reeds and flax, used to relieve the pain. She placed the moistened herbs on the Hebrew woman's abdomen, then began to gently massage her feet. Gradually the woman's breathing slowed. Shiphrah stayed by her side as the labor continued. Between contractions, the woman chanted a Hebrew prayer. Slow and rhythmical. Tender like a lullaby, over and over again:

Patachnu sha'arayich
Bo'i, bo'i
Bi lech taych al ha yi or
Na chin li vo ayich.

"As you journey down the river,
We make ready for your presence.
We have opened the gates.
Come in, come in."

Patachnu sha'arayich
Bo'i, bo'i
Bi lech taych al ha yi or
Na chin li vo ayich.

Shiphrah knew enough of the language to understand the words. The midwife was deeply moved by the
woman's strength and the beauty of her song. She felt
drawn into the rhythm and the sinuous melody.

A sudden cry interrupted the song. The laboring
woman raised herself up on her elbows, threw her head
back, and grunted as if expelling a powerful breath.
"Auaggh!" Shiphrah recognized the familiar utterance
as that of a woman pushing new life into the world.

"Let me help you up," she said as she guided the
Hebrew woman to her feet, supporting her in a deep
squat and positioning her feet solidly on two flat stones.
"Your child will come soon."

The woman groaned; her body shook with the
effort. Shiphrah reached out her hands and felt the
baby's velvety head emerging. *If it is a boy, kill him.* She
tried to imagine the act, tried to imagine cupping her
hand over the baby's face. But she couldn't. She couldn't
force her mind consider it. Instead, she was filled with
the song: "We have opened the gates, come in, come in."

Over and again it reverberated inside her, until
even she began to sing the prayer aloud.

Another forceful contraction and the baby's head
was in her hands. Eyes wide open. Newborn baby, child
of slaves, locked eyes with Shiphrah, the Egyptian midwife.

Poised to kill and trembling with fear, Shiphrah felt as if she were being drawn into a narrow chasm. With steep walls on either side, she was swept down into a watery darkness. Helpless to resist the raging current, she was tumbled and thrown. *What power is this that shakes me limb to soul?*

"I AM WHO I AM." The divine words pulsed through her, slamming her down, spinning her around in the turbulent swirl. "Do not do this thing that Pharaoh has commanded, for it is evil." The torrent dragged her deeper and deeper into darkness and despair. And then, as suddenly as it began, the churning ceased. Everything was still, as if she had arrived in a calm pool. "Do not fear, Shiphrah, for I am with you."

The moment passed with the familiar slush of warm fluid as the newborn slipped easily into her hands. She cradled the baby close to her chest. Joy and relief held her like an invisible hand. She softly kissed the newborn's forehead and whispered, "Welcome. Welcome to this world." Her face washed with tears, she carefully placed the child into the arms of the Hebrew woman, saying, "Mother, you have a son!"

ABOUT THE STORY

Archaeology tells us much about the history of ancient Egypt. We know very little, however, about the Hebrew enslavement, except for the stories told in the biblical books of Genesis and Exodus.

Biblical scholars debate whether Shiphrah was Hebrew or Egyptian. This is the story of an Egyptian Shiphrah: a woman of modest means, not part of the oppressed people herself—someone who would have had to look outside herself to find compassion for the scorned Hebrew people.

B. W.

A DANCE IN THE DESERT

*So Miriam was confined outside the camp for seven days,
and the people did not start out again until she was
brought back.*

—Hebrew Bible, Numbers 12:15

M iriam, how do we know what God wants of us,
this mighty God of Sarah, Rebecca, Rachel, and
Leah?"

Miriam turned to the young woman who questioned her. Wiping the sweat from her forehead, she
shifted to ease the soreness in her tired muscles and
aged joints.

"This Covenant I speak of is not too baffling for
you, nor is it beyond your reach," she said, looking one
by one at the women who sat in the shade of her tent
flap. They had listened to her teaching all afternoon. "No,
it is very close to you, in your mouth and in your heart,"
Miriam told them. "And it is you who will mother a new
generation of Israel in the Promised Land."

If this wandering in the wilderness ever ends, she
thought.

Miriam brushed that thought aside and stood. It was time for the evening meal. She lifted her tambourine overhead, moving her feet in a slow rhythm. The women joined her, forming a circle, their voices rising together in song, their bodies moving in praise of Shechinah, She the Holy-One-Who-Dwells-in-This-World.

When they had left, Miriam sank to her mat, giving in to her aching fatigue. She sat, dozing, until she heard the footsteps of Moses and Aaron. A quick look at their faces told her that her brothers were bickering. *This time, I will not be drawn into it.*

But once they had seated themselves, she caught Moses eyeing the dead fire under her cooking pot. The heat, her weariness, past hurts—all mingled and prickled the back of her neck. She was more than just a cook and tent sweeper.

"I suppose you're looking for supper," she said.

"N…n…no." He avoided her eyes.

"Moses, we are God's Chosen People," she said. "Sometimes you act as if you are the Chosen *One.*"

He didn't answer. But as usual, Aaron had plenty to say.

"It's not just you who speaks for the Lord, Brother. Miriam and I also know the Holy One. We, too, are capable of leading the people in the Lord's ways."

Moses opened his mouth to reply, but Miriam cut him off. "If not for my quick thinking, you'd never have seen your first birthday. You'd have drifted to the sea in that basket instead of being adopted by Pharaoh's daughter."

"If not for my quick tongue, we'd all still be in Egypt making bricks," said Aaron. "You'd never have been able to argue our case with Pharaoh, the way you stammer."

The wind gusted and Miriam threw up her hands to guard her eyes from blowing sand. The goatskin flap overhead nearly ripped from its lacings.

"Come out, you three, to the Tent of Meeting," said a voice, booming like thunder, yet with such quiet Miriam heard it most loudly in her heart.

Recognizing the voice of the Almighty, she gasped and bowed her head to the earth.

The wind died and she struggled to her feet, leading her brothers to the place. She dared not look at the column of cloud that descended before them.

"Listen to me," came the voice of the Lord. "Why do you quarrel like jealous children? I reveal myself to whom I please, in the way I please. I've heard enough of your criticism and complaints."

The Lord's anger raged like a runaway fire. Miriam pulled herself into a ball against it, but the heat seared her flesh. As quickly as it had come, the anger was gone. Stillness returned, and Miriam opened her eyes.

Straightening her limbs, she saw Moses staring at

her, mouth gaping. Aaron, too, looked stricken. He grabbed Moses by the shoulders.

"We've been foolish! Sinful! Moses, do not hold it against us. Not against Miriam." He dropped to his knees.

"Please, Lord...." Moses stretched his arms to the heavens and wailed. "Heal her, I pray."

Miriam wheeled around. What did they mean? Her gaze fell to her hands. A white, scaly rash covered them.

Her breath caught in her throat, and a soft moan was the only sound she could make. She felt her cheeks, her neck—she lifted her tunic to see her feet and ankles—the rash was everywhere.

The voice of the Lord sounded again. "Moses, I refuse your prayer. This will give you all some time to think."

Miriam knew the Lord's command about skin rashes. She would have to spend seven days outside the camp. Seven days separated from her people. *One more trial in these endless years in the desert.* Yet, she had survived so far. Turning on her heel, she marched away.

At her tent she collected her sleeping mat, a water skin, and a packet of dates and figs. She could gather manna, the food God sent from heaven each day, outside the camp just as easily as within. Without a word, she trudged between fire pits and playing children until she left the dwellings behind.

Miriam settled herself in the shadow of a tower of shale jutting up from the barren ground. She rested her head and folded her empty hands. Her heartbeat had slowed to a peaceful pace. Noticing how it kept time with the dance of heat waves in the distance, she smiled. Then she slept.

She opened her eyes to darkness and a sky filled with stars. Shivering, Miriam stood and stretched her cramped legs. "I'm getting too old for this," she muttered. "Aching bones, the grit of sand always in my mouth, and now blistering sores. Lord, why me?"

Sitting down again, she pulled her tunic tightly around her. The Lord was silent.

"I'm famous for my healing, Lord. People gather to hear my wisdom. I've never been cast out."

In the western sky a single star fell, its path a streak of light. Miriam lifted her hands. "Am I not a prophetess?" she said to the stillness. "Do I not lead Your people in celebration and praise of Your greatness?"

"Miriam."

The voice brushed her ears, tender as a mother's touch. "I love you just as much as I love your brothers."

You've a fine way of showing it, she thought. A chuckle came in reply, more a breeze across her cheek than a sound. She tossed her head, as if she were still angry, but felt all her resistance melting in the nearness of Shechinah.

"Did you not hear your brothers crying out in your defense, and yet I ignored their prayers? They will see how all the people mourn your absence. Not a man or woman will move a step forward without you." Settled again in the shelter of the rock, she drifted to sleep with the words of the Holy One in her ears.

Miriam soon grew impatient with her days of solitude. She knew her sores would not kill her, for she had nursed many cases of leprosy these years in the desert. Searching the rock for shady crevices that captured the dew, she found enough healing plants to make a soothing poultice for her itchy skin.

On the fifth day, as the sun reached its zenith, shrinking any shade to a sliver, she paced the sand. Taking a vicious swat at a fly buzzing about her face, Miriam again called out.

"*El Ro'i,* God Who Sees—" Miriam used the name that the outcast Hagar had given the Lord. "I chafe at such idleness. *El Ro'i,* surely you have more important things for me to do than sit here and sweat?"

"Ahh…. My Miriam, never afraid to speak her mind."

"Did you not give me a mind to think, a tongue to speak?"

"Yes, I did. But your blessing can also be the rock in your path."

Miriam knew the Lord's words were true, but she wasn't in a mood to hear them. She lifted her water skin and took a swallow of the tepid water, but it did nothing to dampen her irritation. It had been so many long years since they left Egypt. She was an old woman now.

"I'll never see the Promised Land," she wailed aloud. Miriam fell to her knees, dropping her head to the ground. Numb to the grit, heedless of the sores on her face, she wept into the hot sand.

"I'll die in this desert." Her fingers clenched around sand and bits of rock. "My bones will be dust in an alien land." Miriam rose to her feet and flung the stuff away with all her strength.

"Why, Lord?" She grabbed another stone and hurled it against the tower of rock that had been her shelter.

"Why?" She threw stone after stone. They clattered as they hit, shattering, splintering the quiet of the heat-laden air. When her hands could find no more stones, she ran after those she'd thrown and pounded her fists against the shale tower until she collapsed on the ground, her anger spent.

Trembling, Miriam lay panting for breath. "Shechinah—" Her lips formed a silent plea. As the sun made its slow journey toward the west, she let go, bit by bit, of all she'd held so tightly.

As the heavens are high above the earth, Shechinah, so are your ways high above my ways.

The sky blazed orange and the sun sank. *I have stilled my soul, hushed it like a weaned child.*

The song of bubbling water revived Miriam. By the light of the stars, she saw that a well had sprung up close by. Giving thanks to the Lord, she rose and washed her bloodied fists, then drank her fill.

On the sixth day, water from the well formed a pool, and Miriam bathed. She did not speak to the Lord and did not hear the Lord's voice. But on the seventh day, her skin glowed with health, clear as the flesh of a newborn babe. She started back to camp.

The jingle of tambourines met Miriam's ears before she could see the tents. With hands clapping and colorful banners waving, the women came out to meet her, singing. As she approached, Miriam saw Moses and Aaron among them.

They pulled her into the circle of dancing. Her feet light as a young girl's, her heart beating as if with first love, Miriam joined in the song of praise. Together with her people—the People of God—she danced until the bitterness blended with the sweet.

ABOUT THE STORY

Miriam first appears in the Bible in the second chapter of Exodus. Pharaoh has commanded that all Hebrew male infants are to be killed, and Moses' mother plots to save her baby boy. Miriam is not mentioned by name, but when Moses' mother puts him in a basket among the reeds of the Nile, his sister stands guard to see what will happen. Pharaoh's daughter discovers Moses and wants to adopt him. Miriam quickly steps out and offers to find a wet nurse for the baby.

Moses' older sister next appears years later when the Israelites escape from Egypt. In Exodus 15:20 she is called the prophetess Miriam, and she leads the women in music and dancing to praise God and celebrate the Israelites' salvation from the Egyptians.

Although Miriam probably continued her leadership role in the community, she is not mentioned again in the Bible until the events of this story, where she is struck with "snow-white scales," sometimes translated as "leprosy." It's doubtful that her skin rash, from which she recovered, was the Hansen's disease we think of today when we hear the word leprosy. Like Moses, Miriam also died before reaching the Promised Land. She was buried at Kadesh. Jewish sources describe "Miriam's Well" as an unending source of water that followed the people throughout their desert sojourn for as long as Miriam was with them.

M. C. F.

THE POOL OF SILOAM

Go, inquire of the Lord for me, and for the people, and for all Judah, concerning the words of this book that has been found.
—Hebrew Bible, 2 Kings 22:13

Huldah knelt next to the deep pool of water, entranced by the way it warmed her face in the first light of morning. She felt the reflected beams dance across her cheeks. Will the Lord bless me today so that I can feel him, too? *This is the day I need to hear you, Lord; this is the day I need to feel you.*

Last night, under midnight's screen, King Josiah's priests had come to her home and delivered a large scroll found by the workmen repairing the Jerusalem Temple. Huldah shivered as she remembered how Hilkiah, the high priest, had barged in, startling her awake. He needed answers—the king wanted the prophetess to determine if the scroll was authentic. Were these the real words of Israel's God? Had Israel broken its Covenant with God? Were the Israelites now cursed?

It was the finest scroll she had ever seen, a large hide scraped and tanned until it was supple as silk, ivory in color. After the priests had left, Shallum, her husband, had stood beside her, helping her unroll it. Even in the oil lamp's subdued light, the scroll glowed, and the intricate beauty of the sacred writing left them both speechless.

The scroll was too important to the king—to all Israel—for Huldah to read in last night's half-sleep. *This is why I came to the pool, to prepare myself for God's answers,* she told herself, looking at her reflection in the water. Her long, white braid was hidden from view but she felt its comforting weight down her spine. Her skin was old, yes, wrinkled and tan as a dried fig, but her hazel eyes glimmered with the same sparkle as the water.

She gently laid a jug on the water's surface, then pressed on the base, watching and controlling the water as it spilled over the lip into the jug. She listened as the water filled the jug, its music starting at a hollow note lower than her husband could sing, until the almost-full jar sang the sweet, high song of a child. Closing her eyes, she could always hear the exact note that signaled the jar at its fullest. *This is how I also listen for God— patiently waiting for answers and, when they come flowing in, knowing when the exact note of truth is reached.*

Huldah heard the steady steps of a donkey and the encouragement of its boy-master approaching the reservoir. "Good morning, grandmother." She heard the greeting a young man used to address a woman her age.

Huldah opened her eyes from her reverie and

gasped. She saw a boy's body lying limp and twisted, half in the water and lifeless. His torn and bloodied tunic exposed a sword cut to his chest. Beside him lay the donkey, its throat slit and its carcass draped on a flat, poolside rock. A small stream of blood seeped from its neck to the water.

In a moment the image vanished before the prophetess's eyes, but not in her heart. She tensed.

"Grandmother, I did not mean to startle you so," said the boy standing before her.

"Oh." Huldah paused and caught her breath. "It was only an old person's daydream," she said. "I must have been half-asleep. Perhaps it is lucky that you woke me before I fell into the water." She forced a smile.

Curious, for the boy spoke with an accent, she said, "I see you have jars that your donkey has carried a long distance. Where are you from?"

"We have just come from the north. It is too dangerous to stay there any longer. First my great-grandfather lost his grazing lands to the Assyrians, and now my father is afraid to stay because there are rumors that another great kingdom to the north grows mighty and greedy."

Huldah flinched with this news. The Kingdom of Judah was indeed vulnerable and her task more pressing. "So you have come to Jerusalem to make your new home?"

"Grandmother, we have no choice. We have cousins here, and they have promised to let us share in their linen-weaving business."

"Well, welcome to you, and may God bless you and help your family prosper."

It is time, past time, to read through the scroll. Huldah lifted her full jar out of the water and stood it upright on the bank. She pulled out the cotton cloth tucked in her robes, wrapped it firmly around her head, and placed the jar atop.

As she climbed back up the stairs leading to the city, she could sense the quiet solace of the early morning streets. But when she turned the first corner, she stopped: Death had visited. The quiet was the silence of the dead. Strewn everywhere were the bodies of men she recognized. Lifeless women lay over their babies in hopes of protecting them from sword blows. Market stalls were overturned, and the unblinking eyes of shopkeepers stared skyward.

A guttural moan escaped from Huldah's throat. "Adonai, what are you trying to tell me?" she whispered. She closed her eyes and waited. *Courage. Courage.*

Slowly, Huldah reopened her eyes. The bodies were gone. Two chickens pecked for food, while a dog snuffled through garbage in the dawn hour. The small buildings lining the west side of the street mirrored the peach hues of sunrise.

She took off at a brisk pace, her heart racing from the vision of catastrophe. It wasn't too far to her quarter of Jerusalem—still a manageable climb for a grandmother.

By the time Huldah reached her home, Shallum, her husband, stood waiting for her in the doorway, an anxious expression on his lean face.

"Huldah!" he exclaimed, "The priests, Hilkiah and three others, have already come back this morning. They want answers. King Josiah is distraught and pacing about the halls of his palace. He has tried to cleanse Judah of false gods, but perhaps not fast enough. Everyone is impatient for you to get to work and say if these curses will come true!"

Huldah brought both hands to the water jug, steadying it. Without answering her husband, she lifted the jar off her cloth turban and then carefully lowered it to the floor.

Huldah was a name that meant "having the qualities of a ferret," signifying her ability to get to the hidden truth of any situation, as well as a fierce temper. This time she caught herself before she responded in anger. "I cannot demand that God give me answers exactly when and where a priest—or even a king—demands it. Did you not tell them so?" she asked.

"I am just the king's tailor. When he says sew, I sew. When he says make his wives ten gowns, I make ten gowns. When his priests ask for answers, I get them.

Huldah, you know we must do the king's bidding when he asks—we depend on him for our very bread."

Letting silence come between her words and Shallum's, Huldah waited before speaking. The water jug brought back to mind the memory of the morning. "I have prepared myself the best I know how."

She began to fix herself a small breakfast of milk and bread. "I'll eat and then go study the scroll. It may take me a day, or it may take me a week. But the timing is not up to me. If the scroll contains God's own words for the people of Israel, we will know." She reached for the bread and tore off a piece. She pulled the jug of milk off the table. "Please, Shallum, tell the priests this if they come back today: I must remain silent and undisturbed."

She held his gaze for a few long moments. He looked distraught; fending off the priests was now his job. Huldah knew he would dread this. He would be extremely nervous until the moment she was ready to speak again. But, for now, he turned away and let her eat in silence. He busied himself with measuring some silks and wools that had arrived several days ago for the king. *May God give us both courage.*

Having finished her meal, Huldah climbed the stairs to the rooftop. She would not eat again until God blessed her with answers. She would drink water only, and that from the Pool of Siloam alone.

She gazed east, toward the Temple. *Where exactly had the scroll been found, and how old was it?* Walking over to the parapet, she looked below. Children helped with chores, merchants arranged their wares, and customers already were bickering over prices. Inhaling deeply, she caught the aroma of baking bread.

Huldah walked away from the edge, leaving the noise behind. She pushed aside the flaps from the two ends of her tent, fastening them above. It would give her more light to read by, as well as welcome ventilation.

She had placed the clay jar of cool water in the shade of the tent. She took a sip and renewed her pledge to listen patiently. She unrolled the scroll, laying it carefully on her table. Then she began to read:

These are the words that Moses spoke to all Israel beyond the Jordan in the wilderness.... This is the law that Moses set before the children of Israel...

Huldah's skin prickled with the force of these words. Here it was for the first time: the legends, the commandments, and the laws for the children of Israel, all together. She checked herself; her fingers must not damage the sacred calligraphy, only gently grasp the scroll's border. She read on, taut with anticipation.

Know therefore that the Lord your God is God, the faithful God who keeps covenant and steadfast love

with those who love him and keep his commandments, to a thousand generations....

She rose from her studying after a time and ducked
as she passed under the tent entrance. She paced slowly
along the rooftop, hands clasped behind. In learning
how to read, she had seen some of these stories, but not
all. She had been taught the Ten Commandments and
many of the prescribed rituals and laws. *But whose hand
had written these words? What prophet had known all these
things? Could this be anything but the word of God?* She
still wasn't sure. A slight breeze broke the day's heat. She
went back into the tent and continued to read, inhaling
the words, repeating them over and over before moving
on to the next verse.

The day passed without her being aware of it. In
the afternoon, gusts of wind lashed the rooftop tent.
She fastened the door flaps to protect the scroll. Other
than that, she hardly noticed. She drank from her water;
she listened for something inside her.

When she reached the curses inscribed in the
scroll, the words leaped off of the page into her body. It
was the approach of completion, the high note sung by
the water.

Behold, I set before you this day a blessing and a
curse: the blessing, if you obey the commandments
of the Lord your God, which I command you this

day, and the curse…if you go after other gods that you have not known.

Huldah dashed outside her tent, turning toward the Jerusalem Temple as if it were a beacon. From its highest point, black smoke fumed and billowed, blocking out the sun. A cacophony of fierce shouts and wails streamed from behind the Temple walls. The mournful keening of a dozen women surrounded her. Huldah wanted only to cover her ears and shut her eyes. Instead, she bowed her head. She waited for the vision to subside, the voices to quiet. *Adonai: I hear, I see.*

When she finally looked up again, sooty thunderclouds drifted toward the city from the west, piling to remarkable heights. As she remembered the words, Huldah's own fear of God was palpable to her—a hard fist pressing on her breastbone. "*Cursed shall you be in the city, and cursed shall you be in the field.… Cursed shall be the fruit of your body, and the fruit of your ground.… The Lord will cause you to be defeated before your enemies.… A nation that you have not known shall eat up the fruit of your ground and of all your labors.*"

Huldah's scalp tingled and stung. Again and again, she had been shown this bleak future. Returning to the tent, she read through to the last word, even though she knew how the scroll would end.

Huldah looked up from the scroll and stared blankly ahead. *We have broken the Covenant, just as it says.*

Even in our own temple we have allowed children to be sacrificed to Molech and trees worshiped for Asharah.

When at last she felt Hilkiah standing beside her, she recoiled, her deep trance of prayer broken. Tears flooded her eyes. But confident now in the Lord's message, she held the high priest's gaze. "Thus says the Lord," she intoned, "behold, I will bring evil upon this place and upon its inhabitants…because they have forsaken Me and have burned incense to other gods."

The high priest, despite his rank and stature, crumpled to his knees. He bowed his head and listened in silence.

"But as to King Josiah," she continued, "who sent you to inquire of the Lord…because his heart was penitent, and he humbled himself before the Lord…he shall not see all the evil that the Lord will bring upon this place."

After Huldah spoke, the silence seemed to swell between them. Neither spoke; they let the force and truth of the prophecy linger.

"It is certain, then, that the scroll is God's own truth?" Hilkiah finally asked.

"It is a certainty I fear for the children of Israel, for we have allowed abominations to take place in our Temple." She got up and went outside the tent, looking slowly from the scroll toward the Temple. There was nothing to be done now but for King Josiah and all of Israel to renew the Covenant with God.

The sky had turned a seamless teal-blue as the first stars revealed themselves; the horizon shone golden with the last light of day. Hilkiah followed her outside. He watched her and waited.

Unmoving, firm in the words and visions that had been given to her, Huldah felt complete. "There is also security and comfort for our people in this scroll," she said, looking at the Temple and then at Hilkiah. "Israel is now a people of the book. Even if we lose our land, even if we suffer greatly, God's commandments and the Covenant will sustain us."

Buttery light from Jerusalem's windows dotted the view from her roof. From the streets drifted the savory smells of supper. She could see one small flame flicker atop the Temple. *No matter what happens to Judah in the future, no matter who drinks from the Pool of Siloam, this scroll will keep the children of Israel as one, forever. This I know.*

ABOUT THE STORY

Huldah may be the unsung heroine of Judaism, the single most important woman in the history of the religion. Without Huldah's verification of the Book of Deuteronomy in the seventh century B.C.E., Judaism might have disappeared with the next foreign invasion (which came soon enough after the scroll's discovery). Deuteronomy can be viewed as the most complete and unified of any of the Five Books of Moses, so its verification by Huldah allowed the ancient Jewish people to make the remarkable step of creating a portable religion, one not entirely dependent on a special place or temple.

After the Babylonians invaded, the Jewish people did not lose their culture and religion. Huldah's contribution allowed the Judeans to be a "people of the book," with a written code of conduct, commandments, and a covenant with God to unify them always.

S. C.

O COME MY BELOVED

I am a rose of Sharon,
A lily of the valleys.

Like a lily among thorns,
So is my darling among the maidens.

Like an apple tree among trees of the forest,
So is my beloved among the youths.
I delight to sit in his shade,
And his fruit is sweet to my mouth.
                    —Hebrew Bible, *Song of Songs* 2:1–3

*O*n the evening of creation, a bride prepares herself for
    marriage. She bathes in the well of living water. She
wears a gown woven with roses and shoes stitched together
with spun gold. She sings her song of desire; her voice is sweet
like honey. As the dawn light of the first day rolls away the
darkness of night, the divine couple stands together beneath a
wedding canopy, a gleaming huppah of cloud. The bride and
the bridegroom hold out their rings, one to the other, and they
speak of their love.

   "*I am to my beloved as my beloved is to me.*"

But out of their golden rings, a howling north wind blows. The wedding party is frightened and scatters to the four corners of the earth. The petals of the roses are dispersed, one from another. Sparks of ice sweep through the garden of love. Everywhere there is darkness, except for a single candle left burning.

Shoshana and her sisters walked toward home. The young women had worked late in the vineyards, and they were weary from their toils. It was a moonless night, and stars lit their way.

As the sisters walked along the path, they came to a place where the wall surrounding the garden had begun to crumble. Shoshana thought she heard a voice calling her name. Like distant thunder it called to her, so she paused on the trail, gazing out across the meadow, toward the city that lay to the north. She said to her sisters, who were anxious to get home, "You go on without me. I hear someone coming."

"Stay here alone?" the sisters cried. "It's not safe! What if it is a leopard coming into the garden?" But Shoshana would not return with them. Instead she stayed alone, listening.

She peered out into the world beyond the garden, waiting for the voice to return. She could hear only the wind. Cautiously, Shoshana stepped through the crack in the wall. Something beckoned her—she could not tell what. One step followed by another, she set out walking toward the flickering lights of the city called Jerusalem.

She walked steadily along the path that led her up and out of the thicketed lowlands. As she approached the city, a night watchman shouted at her to stop. "Young woman," he called. "What are you seeking?"

"I am seeking my beloved," she replied, "the one that has beckoned me." Amazed at her own words, Shoshana cupped her hand over her mouth, realizing she had spoken the truth.

"You have no business here," said the watchman. "Return to your home at once!"

But Shoshana paid no attention to the man's rough words, and she kept on walking along the road. Angry, the watchman came down out of his tower, took hold of her, and dragged her back to the garden, pushing her through the crack in the wall.

In the morning her sisters found Shoshana lying by the wall where the watchman had left her. Her sisters carried her back to their grandmother's house deep within the garden. They dressed her wounds and put her to bed.

Shoshana tossed and moaned in a feverish sleep. Days later, she awoke just as the sun was setting in the west. She sat up in bed and watched her grandmother take a bit of flame and light a pot of oil that sat on the table. The old woman covered her eyes and recited a melodious prayer:

Dodi li va'ani lo.

"My beloved is to me and I am to him."

When she finished her prayer, the old woman spoke. "You are seeking your beloved, your brother. And he is searching for you."

Amazed that her grandmother could see into her soul, Shoshana asked, "How can I find him when the watchman will not let me search outside the garden?"

"I will teach you how to call him to your house. You must follow my instructions with all of your heart." And so the old woman taught Shoshana the ancient traditions.

In the evening, as the darkness rolled away light, they lit the flame. "Be careful, daughter, that the fire does not go out. It has burned every night since the first day of Creation." Together Shoshana and her grandmother recited the prayers. Their voices blended, the young with the old, like honey with wine. The villagers heard their song and joined in the singing, so that night after night the song grew louder, until at last it pierced the garden wall and could be heard throughout the countryside. Shoshana never tired of singing the prayers. Over and over again, night after night, she was filled with hope. Each time she sang *Dodi li va'ani lo*, it sounded new, as if she were hearing it for the first time.

Now at the same time, a young man known as Ya'ar walked along the road to Jerusalem. Just outside the gates of the city, some merchants had set up their shops, and among them Ya'ar saw a cobbler sitting on a blanket beside the road.

"Please sir," Ya'ar said to the cobbler. "Repair these sandals for me. I have journeyed far to reach this glittering city of kings, and the leather on my shoes is worn through. I should not enter this great city in such disrepair."

The old man picked up the dusty sandals and inspected them. Slowly, he turned them over in his calloused hands, tugging at the leather, rubbing his fingers over the rough places. "You have spent your life dreaming of this highland city."

"And today I will enter Jerusalem! I am so close that I can hear the city noises, and I can smell the savory aroma of lamb roasting in the marketplace." The young man became so excited speaking about all the fine things he would do and see in the city that he became impatient with the old cobbler. "If you would just hurry with your work, I could be on my way."

"As you wish," the old man said. Taking up his needle and heavy thread, he prepared to sew. But before he had made even one stitch, he paused and gazed again at the sandals. "I can easily repair these shoes, but I see that they will not take you to Jerusalem."

"Foolish old man!" Ya'ar cried out in anger. "I am here, at the entrance to the city. Of course I will enter!"

"Yes, I see that you have come all this way. But you have come alone, and you cannot enter without your beloved, your sister whom you have forgotten."

Ya'ar raised his hand as if to strike. "What do you know about me?" he cried.

Undisturbed by the young man's outburst, the cobbler began to sew, piercing his needle through the stiff leather sole. As he did, Ya'ar felt a soothing warmth radiate inside his chest. Time and again the cobbler pushed his needle into the leather and pulled it through, over and again, stitching leather to sole, repairing the shoes. As the cobbler worked, the burning in Ya'ar's chest continued. His clenched fists relaxed, his arms dropped to his side. By the time the old man was finished, Ya'ar's anger had left him; he understood that the cobbler's painful words had been nothing but the truth.

"Tell me, old man, what do you know about my beloved?"

"She is calling out to you. She awaits you in the garden."

Ya'ar looked down toward the valley. The path was obscured by dense forest. Clouds hung over the lush hillsides. The place was mysterious to him. It was the place of his birth, but he had left as a young boy and had never returned, always preferring the high mountain trails.

"I must go into the valley," Ya'ar said, "but tell me, how will I find my way?"

"You will meet many travelers along the way," replied the old man. "Show them kindness, and in exchange they will guide you."

And so Ya'ar thanked the old man and turned toward the valley.

Ya'ar met many people along the way—some old, some young; some rich, some poor; some beautiful, and some ugly. He met a child and carried her across a flowing stream. He met an old woman and gave her his coat. He met a man and listened to his sorrows. And just as the old cobbler had said, the people guided Ya'ar down the meandering path toward the garden, until the day he came to a crumbling stone wall. The sun was beginning to set, so Ya'ar decided to sleep there for the night. Just as he began to search around for some berries to eat, he heard an enchanting song.

It was Shoshana's prayer from within the garden that had reached his ears. A chorus of voices surrounded him with music, but one voice rang clear and strong above them all. *This is the voice of my beloved,* he thought. He walked around the outside until he found a crack in the great, thick wall where he could enter the garden. He began to sing the mysterious song that he heard on the wind:

Dodi li va'ani lo.

"My beloved is to me and I am to him."

Deep within the garden, Shoshana heard Ya'ar's

echoing prayer calling to her, like thunder from the clouds. Trembling inside, she matched the pitch and sang along with the new voice. Still singing, she ran to the edge of the garden, until she reached the place where the wall was crumbling.

Shoshana gazed upon her beloved. And Ya'ar gazed upon her, and their love was a delight between them.

On the evening of the wedding, Shoshana prepared herself for marriage. She bathed in the well of living water. She wore a gown woven with roses and shoes stitched together with spun gold. She sang her song of desire; her voice was sweet like honey.

As the first light of dawn rolled away the darkness of night, the couple stood together beneath a wedding canopy, a gleaming *huppah* of cloud. Shoshana and Ya'ar held out their rings, one to the other, and they spoke of their love.

"I am to my beloved as my beloved is to me."

But out of their golden rings a howling north wind blew. The wedding party was frightened and scattered to the four corners of the earth. The petals of the roses were dispersed, one from another. Sparks of ice swept through the garden of love. The candles flickered and went out. Everywhere there was darkness, except for a single candle left burning.

ABOUT THE STORY

"O Come My Beloved" is a fable inspired by the Song of Songs, a book of biblical poetry that celebrates the love between a woman and a man. The Song of Songs is unique in the Bible in that God is not mentioned anywhere in the text. The Song of Songs also contains no real plot or characters. The use of the terms brother *and* sister *are symbolic and did not mean that the two were actually members of the same family.*

Over the centuries the Song of Songs has been interpreted as a metaphor for the love between God and the people of Israel, between heaven and earth, and between the male and female aspects of God. The love described in the Song of Songs is one of eternal longing. The unnamed couple comes together and then they part again.

In this story a dramatic plot involves the fictional characters Shoshana and Ya'ar (the Hebrew words mentioned in the text for wildflower *and* forest*) and their search for one another. The couple unites, but their wedding is interrupted so that the fable ends in a state of exile, just as it began. The last image is that of a candle left burning, a symbol of the continued longing and the hope that the couple will once again find each other.*

B. W.

RETURN TO HADASSAH

Do not imagine that you, of all the Jews, will escape with your life by being in the king's palace.... And who knows, perhaps you have attained to royal position for just such a crisis.
—Hebrew Bible, Esther 4:13–14

E sther stared in the mirror at the coiffed hair piled high on her head and crowned with a diadem of rubies and sapphires. Oil of myrrh, jars of the best perfumes and spices, and royal gowns awaited her pleasure. As the chosen queen of King Ahasuerus, for five years her every desire had been fulfilled. Except one.

She yearned to return to her youth, when her days were filled with friends' laughter, walks with her mother, visits to the Shushan synagogue with her father. When she was known as the lovely Hadassah, the Jewish girl with the smooth, copper skin and dark hair to her waist.

Removing the headpiece, Esther whispered to the mirror, "Only in the presence of the king will I wear this heavy crown."

In her sitting room, she pulled away the window

curtain and stared out. Her uncle Mordecai walked back and forth in front of the palace. Esther knew her uncle came every day to watch out for her. How she longed to talk to the man who had been her guardian since her parents died of fever. At the palace everyone knew that Mordecai was Jewish, but they had no idea that Esther was also, or that she and Mordecai were related.

Five years ago the king had commanded all young virgins to appear at the palace because he wanted to choose the most beautiful woman in Persia to be his new bride. Mordecai knew that having a Jewish woman so close to the seat of power could help—even save—his people. But he also knew that King Ahasuerus would never marry a Jewish woman, no matter how captivating.

So he had counseled his niece, "From this day on, you will be known as Esther." Mordecai took her right hand and placed it on her heart. "Hadassah can live only here now. If the king chooses you, you will be able to do great things for your people."

Hadassah took a deep breath and smiled. "I'll do my best, Uncle."

Like the other young women, Esther enjoyed the months of pampering in preparation for her audience with the king. Hegai, the man in charge of all the virgins, took a special liking to her and made sure that she prepared herself in ways most pleasing to his king. And when King Ahasuerus finally laid eyes on her, he chose Esther to be his new queen, dismissing all the others.

He doesn't even know me, Esther had thought then. *He doesn't know that Uncle thinks I have a quick wit and a kind heart.* And now, five years later, the king still did not know. He ate and drank with the men and spent his days hunting. He understood little of his lonely queen, who no longer cared about her beauty. A prisoner in the palace, Esther had no contact with her Jewish people.

But Hegai had remained her confidant. That afternoon he delivered her favorite orange spice drink. "How is Her Royal Highness this fine day?"

Esther shook her head. "Not well."

"You have not been well for quite some time. I am worried about you. One of the king's attendants has been praising a special cure. He said he would share it with us this evening in the garden, near the lemon grove."

Esther stared at the older man in confusion.

"Trust me, dear Queen. You won't regret it."

Esther paced back and forth in her chambers until the sun set. At supper she could not eat. Her legs shook as Hegai escorted her out into the garden as darkness fell. Had her silent prayers been answered?

Hegai left her side, and Esther stood for several minutes, looking anxiously into the trees. Finally, when out of the shadows her uncle appeared, she gasped and started toward him, arms outstretched.

Mordecai waved her back. "What a sight you are for my poor eyes, dear Niece. But we must be careful."

Tears streamed down Esther's face. "I do not care, dear Uncle. Please take me away. Our God is not part of this place, and my soul aches for him."

"Esther, Esther," he whispered. "Where would we go? Our people are blessed to have you in such a position of power. Remember when you were crowned, how the king repealed taxes?"

"But they are taxed now. What good am I? I want to be called Hadassah again. I want to live with my people." When her uncle did not answer, Esther turned away. "I thought you would understand."

"I do. Who has not heard of the king's drunken celebrations?" Esther began walking, and Mordecai followed. "But it is what God asks of us."

"Then I am losing faith, Uncle. You uncovered the murder plot against the king and saved his life. But what does King Ahasuerus do? Promotes that horrible Haman to grand vizier instead of you."

Esther heard her uncle's voice harden. "Our time will come. Adonai will see to that." At the sound of echoing footsteps, Mordecai ducked behind the garden wall.

"Don't leave me, Uncle."

"It is not safe. I watch for you every day and pray for you every evening, dear Hadassah."

Later, even the jester with his jokes and tricks

could not lift Esther's heavy heart. Nor could her maidens, who played the lyre and the harp. "Sing with us, Queen Esther. Your voice is like an angel's." She sent them away.

She knew the young women were fond of her, as were the other palace workers. She heard them whispering in the corridors. "Good Queen Esther, she is as kind as she is beautiful."

I am not kind, she thought, as she lay awake that night. *I do nothing for others. My days are filled with empty beauty rituals.*

After midnight, when sleep still wouldn't come, Esther tiptoed out of her chambers and began wandering the marbled floors of the palace, running her fingers along the couches and tables inlaid with jewels of jasper, carnelian, and lapis lazuli. In the great dining hall her stomach lurched at the sight of golden goblets filled with wine and plates filled with sweetmeats.

She sighed as she heard laughter and music waft from the king's quarters. It had been more than a month since he had sent for her at night, and she was relieved. But would he soon be in search of a new queen? Would he send her out on the streets or banish her as he had his beloved wife, Vashti? Esther tightened her robe and ran back to her quarters. Uncle Mordecai had to rescue her before it was too late.

The following afternoon, as Esther walked along

the royal garden path, Hegai approached her. "Your Highness, strange things are happening in front of the palace. Mordecai has refused to bow down to Haman when he enters the palace gates."

Esther gripped the skirt of her embroidered gown and tried to still her shaking hands. Her uncle's refusal to bow to the king's second-in-command could mean death. She must see her uncle again and find out why he was taking such a risk. She looked over at Hegai. Could she trust him? He had helped her win the king's favor. He had arranged the garden meeting with her uncle. How much did he know?

The next morning, Esther left the palace for a ride in her carriage. She instructed the coachman to drive by the front gate. There Mordecai sat, unmoving, his face like a stone. Gone were her uncle's velvet robes, replaced by a sackcloth of camel's hair; his feet were bare, and there were ashes on his head.

When Hegai brought her afternoon refreshments, she whispered to him, "I must see Mordecai." He left without a word.

When he returned to retrieve the tray, he murmured in her ear. "Midnight—lemon grove."

That night, when Mordecai finally emerged from the shadows, Esther could not stop herself from grasping his arm. "Uncle, has someone in our family died? Why are you wearing sackcloth and ashes?"

"Haven't you heard, niece? Haman, in the name of the king, has issued an edict to cleanse Persia of all the Jews."

Esther shook her head. "I hear nothing."

"A decree has been sent out to governors of all one hundred and twenty-seven provinces, demanding the slaughter of every Jew—men, women, and children, young and old." Mordecai spat on the ground. "Haman determined the day of the slaughter by casting *pur*. The lot fell on the thirteenth day of the twelfth month."

Esther covered her face with her hands and wept. "How can the king allow this? Never before has he harmed the Jews. He has always allowed us to practice our faith."

"Now he listens only to Haman. By refusing to bow down to Haman, I forced his revenge."

"That despicable man cares only about his own power." Esther shivered, as she wrapped her silk shawl tightly around her shoulders.

Mordecai looked at Esther. "Only you can save us, by requesting that the king change this royal decree."

Esther turned away. "Why does everyone think I have power because of my beauty? The king has not even called me into his presence for thirty days. You know full well that it is against the law to go unbidden, even for the queen."

"But King Ahasuerus has never favored anyone so

much as you. Your people are wailing and weeping, their lives soon to end. You must help them."

"The king must be as cruel as Haman to allow such a travesty." Esther picked a lemon off a tree and smelled its bitter fragrance. "He adored Vashti. Vashti, his beloved queen, who dared to refuse his command, who would not appear before a drunken king. For that he banished her to the desert, far away from her people." Esther threw down the lemon. "But it would be even worse to appear without his call. For that he could have me killed."

"Do not imagine that you, Esther, of all the Jews, will escape with your life by being in the king's palace. And who knows, perhaps you have attained to royal position for just such a crisis."

"Oh, Uncle. I had no need for courage before this, only a pretty face." Esther's shoulders began to shake.

Mordecai took his niece's hands in his. "You have long been brave, Hadassah. Despite losing your parents and the support of your people, you have survived alone in the palace. It has all prepared you for this, your moment, your chance to be a woman of God. I must go before we are discovered." Mordecai kissed Esther on the forehead. "You are the only hope for your people."

Esther returned to her chambers and blew out her lamp. Maybe Adonai would come to her in the darkness. It had been a long time since she had prayed. Bending down on shaking knees, she bowed her head, confusion and fear swirling around her. Finally she began talking to a God she thought had deserted her. Words from a psalm her mother used to sing leapt to her lips. "From the day I was brought here till now, your handmaid has had no joy except in you, O Lord, God of Abraham. Hear the voice of those in despair. Save us from the power of the wicked and deliver me from my fear."

Esther looked out to the hills as the sun began to rise, and she felt her heart begin to soften. She was not fearless like Mordecai, but she wanted to be. She thought of her parents and their unwavering trust in God. Like Mordecai, they would expect no less of her. Esther walked over and stared into the mirror. *This is my time, my chance to prove that I am more than beauty.*

She must prepare to face her king. But she could not do it alone. By the early morning light, she awakened her maidens.

"Dear Queen," one said sleepily, "it is good to see you smiling again." The three young women arose from their beds. "We will draw a bath for you, filled with the most precious oils. We will wash your soft hair."

"Later. First I must cleanse myself in another way, and I would like you to join me. For three days we will fast. Then we will celebrate." The young women looked confused. To one she said, "Ask Hegai to come to my chambers." To another she commanded, "Go out into the marketplace and bring back four sackcloth garments and ashes from the cooking fire."

To the last she said, "Bring me my quill pen and parchment." When it arrived, Esther wrote out a message.

> Uncle, assemble all the Jews who live in Shushan. Fast in my behalf; do not eat or drink for three days, night or day. My maidens and I will observe the same fast. Then I shall go to the king, though it is contrary to the law; and if I am to perish, I shall perish!

When Hegai appeared, she handed him the folded sheet. "Bring this to Mordecai." Hegai nodded and departed.

Esther directed her maidens to remove her silk garments and then their own. She pointed to the camel's hair garments and they pulled one over her head and then their own. Finally she told them to shake ashes over all their heads. "This is how our bodies will end up," Esther whispered. "Back to ashes." The young women looked confused. Esther beckoned them closer. "You do not know my Jewish faith. But I believe you understand that killing people for their beliefs is wrong." They bowed their heads and knelt by her side.

Hour after hour, Hadassah prayed aloud, reciting the psalms she had learned in childhood and her own desperate prayers. "My Lord, I am alone and have no help but You. Through my own choice, I am endangering my life. Give me courage, King of kings and Master of all power. May my words be persuasive when I face the lion."

As the hours dragged by, Hadassah's skin itched and her body longed for food. She had forgotten what it felt like to go hungry. It helped her to remember how the Jewish people had suffered in the desert and were suffering now.

After three days and three nights, Hadassah stood up and put her arms around her maidens. "Thank you for joining me in my time of need. Now I must prepare for the king."

"We did not know that he had sent for you." The young women looked frightened.

"He has not. But I pray that he will be happy to see me." Esther clapped her hands. "Quickly. Draw my bath. Bring me my finest gown. Lay out my crown."

"Your majesty, you must eat something first. You need strength to face the king."

"My people have fasted three days, too. Their strength is all I need."

Esther's maidens dressed her hair with silk ribbons and clothed her in a robe of finest linen, embroidered with threads of pink and orange, yellow and blue, all the colors of the rainbow. Layers of silk fringe fell from her shoulders. Lastly, they placed the jeweled crown on her head.

"Never have you looked so magnificent, Queen Esther," one whispered.

"Let us pray my inner beauty shines as well." Esther opened the heavy door before she could change her mind.

Hegai stood waiting. "You are radiant, my queen. When I helped you to win over the king, I knew that you were not only beautiful but wise," he whispered, bowing before her.

Her maidens carried her train as Queen Esther proceeded down the corridor toward the throne room. Dozens of men stood in the gallery, hoping for an audience with King Ahasuerus. Murmurs filled the hall as shocked onlookers spotted the unannounced queen.

Esther started to wonder once again what it felt like to die but dismissed those thoughts from her mind. Whispering prayers to herself, Esther willed her legs to move. "O Lord, God of Abraham. Hear the voice of those in despair. Save us from the power of the wicked and deliver me from my fear."

At the entrance to the throne room, Esther stopped, her heart beating as if it were about to burst out of her chest. She gripped the folds of her gown. *If I am to die, I will die. But I will be with my people. I will trust in God.*

With trembling hand, she opened the curtain and stepped inside, her feet anchored to the marble floor.

"What is it, my queen?" the king called out in surprise.

With a deep breath, Esther held up her head and marched forward. It was time the king met Hadassah.

ABOUT THE STORY

King Ahasuerus, moved once again by Esther's beauty, does not have her killed or banished. Instead he offers to honor her any desire. Admitting that she is Jewish herself, Esther requests that her people be saved, and the king agrees. When the king finds out that Mordecai, not Haman, saved his life, Mordecai is installed as the grand vizier. In his new role, Mordecai works to improve the conditions of the Jewish people in Persia.

The Book of Esther encourages Jewish people to remember that even when they are slaves and in exile, God is present in their daily lives. From Esther's story comes the origin of the festival of Purim, which every year commemorates the deliverance of the Jews from their enemies. The name comes from the Persian word pur, *meaning "lot" or "chance," and refers to the lot cast by Haman to determine the best day to carry out his plan to destroy the Jews.*

Esther's physical beauty was unmatched. But like many attractive women, Esther found her beauty to be empty without the love of her family and friends and her faith in God. Her beauty brought her queenship. Her courage brought her freedom.

C. R. M.

CHRISTIAN STORIES

WOMAN TO WOMAN

Elizabeth, filled with the Holy Spirit, cried out in a loud voice and said, "Most blessed are you among women, and blessed is the fruit of your womb."
— *Christian Bible, Luke 1:41–42*

"M y soul magnifies the Lord, and my spirit rejoices in God my Savior," Mary whispered as she walked along the dusty road. Ever since that morning two weeks ago, those words had been emblazoned on her heart.

She paused to breathe in the warm spring air and gazed in gratitude at the cultivated fields and vineyards that once more dotted the land. For eighty miles the caravan had trudged past dry, sunburned hills. Finally, the Holy City beckoned. Mary and her fellow travelers from Nazareth were tired from nearly four days of walking. But as they spotted the huge buildings of Jerusalem, their steps quickened. Mary ran to keep up with her friends.

She knew that crowded streets, hugs from relatives, and aroma of spices in the marketplace would soon invigorate her blood. Right now, however, something else coursed through her veins.

Ruth and Abigail waved at her to come along. "Isn't it exciting?" Ruth called out. "Will we see you in Jerusalem, or will you take all your Passover meals with your betrothed, Joseph?" Her friends' laughter swirled around the thoughts in Mary's whirling mind. She stopped and squinted her eyes. In the midday sun, the Temple looked hazy, like a mirage in the desert. She knew the Temple was real. But perhaps the angel had been a mirage. Maybe she was not carrying a child. Maybe her elderly cousin Elizabeth was not with child, either.

How was she to know? Her mind flashed back to that morning when the angel Gabriel appeared. "Greetings, Favored One," he had said. Mary couldn't believe her eyes. An angel encircled in glowing light stood before her. She'd heard stories at the synagogue about Gabriel, how in the Book of Daniel he had warned people about the end of the world. Thankfully she remembered that he'd also given Daniel wisdom and understanding. But that day he had told her she was to be the mother of God...

Mary's mother, Anne, joined her, as her friends rushed by.

"I thought we should talk again before we reach the Holy City."

"Mother, you've already promised that you would speak to Father about my visiting Cousin Elizabeth for a while."

Anne nodded. "But I've been doing more thinking."

Mary rearranged the linen veil over her long, brown hair and whispered, "You don't believe that I am to be the mother of the Messiah."

Anne rubbed her daughter's shoulders. "No one is more deserving."

Mary took a deep breath and blinked. "Gabriel said that I was not to be afraid. But I am. That's why I *must* go to see Elizabeth. Only then will I know for sure."

The two women began walking again. "Daughter, I know my favorite cousin will take good care of you. But perhaps your father should talk to Joseph about moving up the marriage date."

Mary stared down the road. Mary's father, Joachim, and her betrothed were far in the lead.

"Even though Joseph is kind, you're afraid that he will put me away if he finds out that I am with child."

"We have to consider these things, daughter. How can we expect others to believe—"

Mary strode away. Only fourteen, she had barely started her monthly flows. She was not ready for a baby and marriage. Mary hardly knew Joseph. But she'd heard enough talk over the years. Abigail had told her what one village elder at the well had said last spring. "Mary is lucky that Joseph has chosen her.

He's not young. But she's no great catch, with her father a day laborer and her mother barren until late in life."

Still, her friends weren't betrothed yet, and Mary knew that people thought her pretty. "Your eyes have stories to tell," her grandmother used to say. Mary wished her grandmother were still alive. She'd know how to advise her.

Mary glanced back at her mother trudging along. Her stooped shoulders made her seem so old.

God chose me! Mary picked up a pebble and threw it down the road as far as she could, then waited for her mother. *I wish I could share my news with Ruth and Abigail. But they probably wouldn't believe me if I did,* she thought.

After eight days of Passover festivities, an uncle agreed to escort Mary into the Judean hills where Elizabeth and her husband, Zechariah, lived.

"Stay as long as you need to," Joseph said, taking Mary's hand. *Will he be so understanding when he finds out that I am carrying a child?*

She waved until her family was only a small speck on the dirt road winding north. Then she and her uncle departed with a caravan heading east into the hills.

By noon they had reached the town square. Her uncle pointed up to Elizabeth and Zechariah's home overlooking the village and continued on with the caravan.

After a drink of water from the well of Ein Karem soothed Mary's thirst, she began plodding up the long hill. Moving in slow motion, she felt as if she were walking into a fierce wind, even though the day was calm. Could she already be feeling new life inside her, or was she just tired from traveling?

At the top she glanced northward to the tomb of Samuel. The great prophet's mother, Hannah, had waited all her life to have a child. "Just like me," Mary's mother often said. After Samuel was born, Hannah gave her son over to God's work. *That would be so heart-wrenching,* thought Mary.

Long before she reached Elizabeth's home, Mary spotted her cousin sweeping the courtyard. She stopped, her chest heaving, and strained her eyes but could not tell if her cousin was pregnant.

When Mary entered the gate, she called out to the older woman, who was indeed large with child. Elizabeth exclaimed with a loud cry. "Blessed are you among women, Mary, and blessed is the fruit of your womb. Why has this happened to me, that the mother of my Lord comes to me?"

Tears flowed down Mary's cheeks as she ran into Elizabeth's arms. They stood holding each other for a long time. It was all as the angel had said. When Mary let go, she began moving to and fro, her arms flowing, side to side. Filled with joy, she twirled round and round, sending her doubts away.

In a strong voice Mary didn't know she possessed, she sang out, "My soul magnifies the Lord, and my spirit rejoices in God my savior." Rising on her tiptoes, she lifted her hands to the sky. Bending down to the ground, she whispered, "For he has looked upon his handmaiden's lowliness."

Coming to full height again, Mary continued. "Surely, from now on all generations will call me blessed; for the Mighty One has done great things for me, and holy is his name." Mary bowed her head for a few moments, then looked up and smiled at Elizabeth. She felt light again.

"O dear cousin, I am so honored that you have come," Elizabeth said.

Mary blushed. "We missed you at Passover. But I am so happy for you and Zechariah."

Elizabeth patted her large belly. "I missed you all as well. But after so many years of waiting, I have finally been blessed, too." She put her arm around Mary. "Come inside. You must be hungry from your travels."

After a midday meal of lentils, bread, and dried goat's meat, both women lay down to rest. As Mary closed her eyes, she wondered if Gabriel would visit her here.

He did not. Instead, as the days flew by, Mary felt God speaking to her through Elizabeth, whose every moment seemed holy. Every morning Mary was awakened by Elizabeth's deep laugh. Even though dark shadows circled her eyes and her bones were tired, Elizabeth hummed as she went about her chores. She didn't seem to worry that she was too old to have a baby.

Each day, while Zechariah prayed with the other priests at the synagogue, Elizabeth and Mary spun wool and prepared the meals. Before the sun got too hot, Mary would go down to the community well to fill the jugs with water.

Every afternoon the two women rested. This priest's dwelling was much larger than Mary's parents' one-room home back in Nazareth. Here, Mary had her own room in which to pray and ponder things in her heart.

One afternoon Mary found Elizabeth in the main room sewing, her face luminous. "Join me, dear. Your baby will need garments, too."

Mary nodded but did not take part. Earlier that morning as she kneaded bread, she had thought of times not so long ago when she had run in the hills and played with her dolls made out of straw. Days when she could still be a child.

Mary sat on the floor beside Elizabeth. "Are you not afraid, cousin?"

"I am afraid that I may not live to see my son."

Elizabeth rubbed her belly. "All I ask is that I see with my eyes and feel with my arms this babe who kicks and cries for life. God has taken away my disgrace and blessed me with this son. I must bring him into the world." Elizabeth stopped. "And yet so many die in childbirth."

Mary shivered. Elizabeth reached over and touched her arm. "Not you, dear. Nothing will happen to the Mother of God."

Mary placed her hand on her womb. The Son of God was growing inside her. She looked at Elizabeth's shining eyes. Mary longed to be that happy.

"Why did God choose *me,* cousin?"

"Because you said yes, in spite of your fear." Mary leaned her head against Elizabeth's shoulder. "God does not ask for perfection, Mary. Only your willingness to say yes."

Mary sat up. "But how can any woman be worthy enough to be the mother of God?"

"My soul magnifies the Lord, and my spirit rejoices in God my savior, for he has looked upon his hand-maiden's lowliness." Elizabeth rose and held out her hands to help Mary up. "You sang those words to me the day you arrived. Never have I seen a person radiate such joy."

Mary clasped her hands together, then held them to her chest. "Oh, I did feel full of happiness that day. But now black clouds of doubt fill my mind." Mary sighed. "What if Joseph banishes me when he finds out I'm pregnant? And what about after the birth? I don't know how to be a mother."

"You were raised by one of the best." Elizabeth patted Mary's hair. "God will help Joseph understand."

And so the days passed, the evenings quiet except for the music of Zechariah's mandolin. Mary's spirit grew stronger as her womb grew larger.

One evening they heard news of a caravan passing through, headed toward Nazareth. Mary retreated to her room and began packing her belongings. She barely slept that night: A baby's cry and a husband's voice filled her dreams.

The next morning Mary trembled as she hugged Elizabeth good-bye.

"You will be a wonderful mother, Elizabeth. These past few weeks you have been so kind to me."

"I love you, dear Mary," Elizabeth whispered as she let her cousin go. "Remember. Just as God lives in you, you live in God. He will take care of you."

Smiling, Mary ran down the hill, then stopped and waved. *Yes,* she thought. *Elizabeth is right.* And she prayed for the courage to find joy in each new day, no matter what the future held.

ABOUT THE STORY

Mary of Nazareth has often been portrayed as the perfect woman. This story explores the possibility that she was human, like the rest of us, and had to struggle to find the courage to be the Mother of God in an unbelieving world. Perhaps she found the support she needed not only from God, but from the women who blessed her life, among them Elizabeth; Anne, her mother; and, later, Mary Magdalene, who stood with her at the foot of Jesus' cross.

The Gospel of Luke is the only one to tell of Mary's visit to Elizabeth, although all four gospels record that Elizabeth gave birth to John the Baptist. The well where Mary stopped for water, below Elizabeth's house, is now known as the Spring of the Virgin. It is dedicated to the mothers Elizabeth and Mary and to all women of the Bible.

The Prophet Muhammad, peace be upon him, thought highly of Mary. He believed her to be holy like her son Jesus—not divine but guided by God and committing no sin.

Today thousands of books, shrines, and Web sites are devoted to Mary. People around the world, from many cultures and religions, look to her for spiritual guidance.

C. R. M.

CRUMBS FROM THE TABLE

Yes, Lord, yet even the dogs eat the crumbs that fall from their master's table.
                                    —Christian Bible, Matthew 15:27

In a village by the sea, in the land of Phoenicia, a woman named Eleni cradled her five-year-old daughter in her arms.

"Hush. Hush, Hannah, my sweet," Eleni said, bathed in the dim morning light. Both of them crouched on the earthen floor in a corner of their home, where the girl shook with fright.

Through the window, Eleni could hear the villagers murmur as they hurried by. "Quickly, quickly, the child of this house is cursed."

"*Shh, shh,*" Eleni rocked, calming the cry—like that of a stray cat—which slipped from her daughter's throat.

Eleni turned at the sound of a knock on the door. Her daughter stared wide eyed, arms stretched in front of her as if pushing something away. "It will hurt me!" Hannah cried, possessed by an evil spirit that no one else could see.

Eleni held her child closer. "Please come in," she said. Looking up to see her sister, Rachel, Eleni smiled.

"I have good news," Rachel said. "They say the Galilean is here. The one who healed the lame man. I know you wished he would come...."

"He's my only hope for Hannah," Eleni said, wishing her husband were alive to help her now.

"I will stay with Hannah while you look for Jesus," Rachel said, taking the child into her arms.

"Thank you," Eleni said as she reached for the small pouch of coins stuffed into the roof thatch.

Wrapping her headscarf about her, Eleni first ran to the village well. She asked of the people there, "Have you seen this man, Jesus, son of David?" And they told her he had gone to Tyre.

Eleni followed the donkey path along the sea to Tyre, a breeze cooling her walk. By midmorning she reached the busy seaport. A fisherman bailing out his boat said to her, "Jesus has gone to the cypress grove." Eleni's face fell as the man pointed to the spit of land that curved around the harbor. It would be a long journey on foot.

"Sir, will you bring me there in your boat? I can pay you," she said, extending her palm with three coins.

To this the fisherman replied, "Hardly enough for me to disrupt my work."

Closing her fingers over the money, Eleni watched the fisherman toss more bilge water over the bow.

"Perhaps if you bring me there you will see Jesus your-self. I heard that he once turned loaves of bread and a few fish into enough food for seven villages. Perhaps he will bless your fishing nets…so that they will sag with the weight of your catch."

Eleni saw the fisherman's eyes light up, but whether it was with greed or belief she couldn't tell. He tugged on the rope to draw his boat nearer to the dock where Eleni stood. "There is a skiff builder there I could speak with," he said, opening his hand for Eleni's coins. "Get in," he said gruffly.

Breaking the water evenly with the oars, the fish-erman rowed to the spit of land by midday. With the folds of her skirt gathered in her hands, Eleni ran up the bank from the sandy harbor. The smell of brine mixed with that of myrtle and the fragrant cypress. *Surely Jesus will help my Hannah, even though we are not Jewish,* Eleni thought to herself as she hurried along. *He helps the lepers.*

Within the spaces of shadow and sunlight hewn by tall cypress trees, she caught a glimpse of the figure of a man surrounded by children. The man disappeared through a gate into the courtyard of a local house. Eleni picked up her step. When she reached the courtyard, another young man greeted her.

"Kind sir, I have come to speak with Jesus. Is he here?" she asked.

The man looked at Eleni. From her language he

could tell she was a Gentile. "You are not from here," he said, speaking to her in her own dialect. "Jesus came for rest. He does not wish to see anyone."

"My daughter is ill. I have heard that Jesus heals. She needs his help."

"I am sorry, woman. He does not wish to speak with anyone today. Please go away."

"But my daughter shakes—she cries out in fear!" Eleni took hold of the young man's robes with both hands. "Please, go to Jesus and tell him he must hear me."

The young man brushed off Eleni's hands. "Jesus needs to rest," he said, walking away. Having traveled so far, Eleni refused to give up so easily. She peered through the gate. Fishing nets lay scattered about. Chickens clucked as they pecked at crumbs on the ground. On the far side of the courtyard, children ran in and out of a doorway, flapping and twirling an embroidered curtain hung over the threshold.

In the harbor behind Eleni, rigging ropes clunked on wooden masts as boats rose and fell on laps of waves. Men hoisted crates of wine jugs into the crafts with the deepest hulls—earthenware to be sold in Tyre, Sidon, Galilee, and beyond. Looking out over the water, she saw in her mind an image of her daughter curled up in a ball in the corner of their home. Hannah's eyes were open, but the girl was seeing something not of this world. Demons!

Again Eleni searched the courtyard for the young man to whom she had spoken. She did not know if he had simply dismissed her or if he would take her plea to Jesus. So she decided to follow him. Reaching through the slats in the gate, she unlatched it. The chickens scurried out of her way as she made for the curtained door. *Jesus will rescue Hannah from the evil spirit,* she assured herself as she pushed past the embroidered hanging into the room where he sat.

A look of surprise and then a twinge of irritation flashed across Jesus' face at the sudden intrusion into his privacy. But his reaction did not discourage Eleni from her mission. She recognized the young man sitting beside him, who began to rise. But Jesus gestured to him. "Stay seated," he said. Then Jesus looked at Eleni.

She returned his gaze. *He looks so young for someone blessed with a gift for healing.* "Have mercy on me, Sir, Son of David. My daughter is possessed by demons. I need your help."

His companion said, "Send her away, Teacher. She is badgering us."

Again Jesus lifted his hand, his face weary.

"Woman," he said to Eleni, "I was sent only to the lost sheep of the house of Israel."

Eleni fell to her knees in front of him. "I know I don't belong to the house of Israel. But my daughter…"

Jesus waved his hand, as if to dismiss her. "It is not

fair to take bread from the children and throw it to the dogs."

Eleni flinched. She looked away. Somewhere in the distance she heard an infant wail. *For Hannah's sake I cannot leave here,* she thought. *Surely this is not the same person who preaches "Love thy neighbor as yourself." Is his heart walled in, like this courtyard, with room enough for some but not for others?*

Words leaped from her lips. "Yes, sir, but even dogs can eat the crumbs that fall from their master's table." Jesus exchanged glances with his young friend.

"Your stories fall kindly on the ears of Gentiles, too," Eleni continued.

As Eleni watched, the frown left Jesus' brow. His face filled with delight, like a child who switches from tears to laughter between sobs.

"My good woman, your trust in me is enormous, and I admire your quick wit." The warmth of his smile cradled Eleni, as she had embraced her own child that morning.

"Forgive me," Jesus continued. "It is not right that I ignore the pleas of those in need simply because they are not Jews. Go home now, and you will find your daughter is well."

"I am grateful," Eleni said, stepping backward toward the door, a hand pressed to her breast. Then she hurried through the courtyard. In the fishing boat back to the mainland, a calm spread over her. She knew without seeing her daughter that Hannah had been healed.

ABOUT THE STORY

In the Christian Scriptures (Mark 7:24–30), the woman in this story has no name. The Gospel of Matthew's version of the story (15:21–28) portrays a Canaanite woman who shouts at Jesus, badgering him for help. As written here, Eleni's story explores a woman who—driven by love for her child and by faith in Jesus as a healer—relies on tenacity and intellect to achieve her aim.

What is striking about this story is that it shows us Jesus' willingness to listen to, and learn from, a nameless woman at a time when female voices were seldom heard. Thus he turned his gaze, as she implored him, upon the wider community of people in need, not only the Jewish people. This story also shows us the human Jesus—one who could make mistakes and correct them with grace.

M. N. S.

WILL I DRINK OF HIS CUP?

Jesus said, "You will indeed drink of my cup, but to sit at my right and at my left is not mine to give but is for those for whom it has been prepared by my Father."
—*Christian Bible, Matthew 20:23*

Hundreds of people crowded the grassy hillside. Even though the midday sun burned hot and flies buzzed in the air, no one moved about, not even the children. Salome sat and listened to Jesus' melodic voice. "Ask, and it will be given you; search, and you will find; knock, and the door will be opened."

Her sons, James and John, stood nearby. Strong and tall, their dark hair brushing their shoulders, any mother would be proud to call them her own.

These boys of mine believe that this man is the Messiah for whom we have waited so long, the one promised us in the Scriptures. All my life the Romans have trod down on us. I want to believe, too. But his words sound so simple and he does not look like a man of position.

Without any warning, three years ago James and John had put down their nets and followed Jesus.

"Mother, Father, we are two of his chosen ones, his disciples now," they had explained.

Her husband, Zebedee, had pounded his fist on the table. "What can a poor carpenter's son from Nazareth know about life? We make a good living with our boats. How can you walk away from that?" Zebedee yelled, glaring at his sons.

But they were Salome's sons, too, and like her they yearned for more.

One day, when Jesus was preaching from a boat on the Sea of Galilee, she went to find out for herself. Zebedee refused to come along. That afternoon Jesus told the story of the brother who had sinned. "We must love and forgive those who have sinned against us." Such an idea Salome had never heard.

Her sons and their childhood friends, the brothers Simon Peter and Andrew, returned home to Capernaum with her for supper that night. On the way, they talked about Jesus' ideas.

"Mother," James said, "the law should no longer be 'an eye for an eye,' as we were taught in synagogue."

Salome shook her head, for she did not understand.

Later, while they were eating, Zebedee once again begged them to return to the family business.

"Father," John said, "we are now fishers of people, in Jesus' name."

Zebedee coughed and then sputtered, "And what will fill your stomachs?"

"Jesus' words feed our souls, Father. He says that God will take care of all our needs."

Simon Peter touched Zebedee's arm. "Don't despair, sir. They are still your sons. Jesus calls these two the Sons of Thunder."

Salome couldn't help but smile. Over the years they'd had plenty of storms around the table.

Now Zebedee was gone, cold in the grave. Because of his hard work, she was not dependent on the charity of relatives or the daily labors of her sons. Now she could listen to Jesus as much as she liked and discover for herself why James and John loved him so. She could make sure, for Zebedee's sake, that her boys were well taken care of.

Salome stood up and stretched her legs, then moved toward the front of the crowd. She wanted to be part of the better world Jesus promised. *Do not the prophets say that all of us chosen people, not just the wealthy, will be saved by the Messiah?*

A woman brought a girl and a boy up out of the crowd. Salome overheard the mother ask Jesus to bless her children. James and John stepped forward to stop the woman. But Jesus waved them away. "Let the children come to me, and do not prevent them; for the kingdom of heaven belongs to such as these."

Salome's throat was parched, but her water pouch was empty. *Why does Jesus dismiss my sons like that?* she wondered. *James and John are his leaders. They preach his word and anoint the sick in his name.*

Salome's eyes flicked back and forth between Jesus and her sons. Jesus had taken the children on his knees, bouncing them up and down and making them smile. When James and John were young, they would have loved a father like that. Never before had she witnessed children recognized by a rabbi in public. In the synagogue young people were taught to sit quietly and listen until they were grown. And women were never allowed to study with the rabbi.

But Jesus put his hand on the young mother's shoulder and spoke to her. *I wish I had known Jesus when I was a child,* Salome thought.

Salome stood up and walked toward him, thoughts filling her mind. *He will talk to me. He said, "Ask and it will be given." He will look out for my sons. James and John were two of the first disciples to be chosen. They are beloved by Jesus and deserve an important place in his new kingdom. I must do this for Zebedee.*

Salome's breath came quickly as her feet carried her to Jesus. But before she could reach him, a handsome youth in rich garments called out. "Teacher, I have followed your commandments. What else must I do to gain eternal life?"

No, tell us about the here and now, Salome wanted to shout.

Jesus stared at the young man. "Sell what you have and give to the poor and you will have treasure in heaven. Then come, follow me."

The youth shook his head and walked away. *My boys have not walked away.*

James and John and the other disciples began whispering among themselves. But it was Peter who spoke up. "We have given up everything and followed you, Lord. What will there be for us?"

Yes, thought Salome. Peter had read her thoughts. She closed her eyes so that she could focus on every word of Jesus' answer.

"Everyone who has given up houses or brothers or sisters or fathers or mothers or children or lands for the sake of my name will receive a hundred times more, and will inherit eternal life."

Salome smiled inside. *My sons will be rich.*

Jesus continued. "But many who are first will be last, and the last will be first."

The last will be first and the first will be last? This has never been so. Salome moved between her sons and put her arms through theirs.

The boys walked their mother over to Jesus. Salome smiled and bowed her head.

"Mother of James and John, what do you wish?"

"My sons have chosen to sit by your side here on earth. They have renounced their father's work and given up their inheritance." James and John tightened their grip on Salome's arms and tried to lead her away.

Salome refused to move. *I am their mother. I must speak for them.* "Declare these two sons of mine will sit, one at your right and one at your left, in your kingdom."

"You do not know what you are asking." Jesus turned to James and John. "Are you able to drink the cup that I am about to drink?"

They answered together. "We are."

Salome stepped back. *Would her sons agree to anything for his approval?*

Jesus put his arms around James and John. "My cup you will indeed drink, but to sit at my right and at my left is not mine to give. It is for those for whom it has been prepared by my Father."

Jesus then turned back to Salome. But she had already moved up to the top of the hillside. There she gazed down at Jesus and the disciples gathered around him. Her boys were smiling. *They love this man. But they are too young to know that love involves not only joy, but sacrifice and suffering, too.*

Yet she did not want to die bitter like her husband.

Could she love like Jesus? Could she, too, drink his cup? The Romans did not trust him. Anything could happen. But he showed no fear.

Salome held out her hands, cupped them around an imaginary vessel, and began to drink. Still she was afraid—of sickness, of violence, of poverty. Salome stopped and stared up at the sky. "Not just of this earth," Jesus had said.

She wanted to know his Father. She yearned to love him like her sons did, to trust that he could show them all a new way to live. Salome breathed deeply and looked down at Jesus. The crowd had dispersed. Jesus and her sons were gathering up their packs and walking away. Salome began running down the hillside. *Yes,* she shouted in her heart. *I will drink with you, too.*

ABOUT THE STORY

A similar story is told in the Gospel of Mark (10:35–45), but in that version James and John themselves ask to sit by Jesus' side. Matthew's version shows us the mother's need to be assured that her sons would be secure for life, contrasted with what Jesus tells us in that story. The choice to love God, in joy and in sorrow, must be made by each human being.

Matthew's Gospel drew many parallels to the Hebrew Scripture. There, the drinking of the cup represents the Jewish people's acceptance of the new Covenant. Salome was concerned for her sons. But they could take care of themselves. It was her own covenant with God that Jesus asked her to consider.

Matthew's inclusion of the mother in his story and later at Jesus' crucifixion shows that Jesus' ministry included women. Because the mother is not named, she represents the thousands of unknown people who followed Jesus, encouraging us to place ourselves in her situation. Since Mark in his Gospel lists a woman named Salome as being present at the crucifixion, the mother in this story is called by that name also. It is possible that Salome was actually the mother of James and John, the sons of Zebedee. We will never know. But we can each live her story in our own way.

C. R. M.

SERVANT TO TRUTH

Now Peter was sitting outside in the courtyard. A servant girl came to him and said, "You also were with Jesus the Galilean." But he denied it before all of them, saying, "I do not know what you are talking about."
—*Christian Bible, Matthew 26:69–70*

B inah straightened her aching shoulders and looked down at her throbbing fingers. Even in the dim light of the big kitchen, she could see they were wrinkled as a crone's skin and raw from rubbing sand against the dirty pots and bowls. As a servant in the high priest's lavish home, she worked from dawn to dusk. Squeezing her hands together to numb the pain, she muttered an oath.

"*Sshh!*" The new girl, Rebecca, had just returned from the great hall with another tray piled high with plates and goblets. "Binah—" she said in a hoarse whisper. "You dare to blaspheme—and on this, the night of Passover."

Binah felt the anger and disappointment of the last year rising in her like a tide of sour wine. "This house is an abomination," she said. Rebecca put down her tray and stood staring. Her eyes were big, her mouth round as the opening of a water jar.

"Shut your lips," Binah snapped. "You'll be catching flies." She directed Rebecca to take her place scrubbing while she sat nearby on a stool.

"My father should never have sent me away from our village," said Binah. "He believes this house is pure, that my service here will make me holy." She reached out to shove a stack of dirty plates within Rebecca's reach. "But Caiaphas is no true high priest. He cares for nothing but his pleasure and power. He lives like a king while taking the food from the mouths of widows and orphans."

The other girl turned her back and hunched over her work, but Binah could not stop the torrent once it had begun. "The poor, the sick, those slaving like us— God promised to save, but there's no justice. Why, oh why, did my father send me to this den of thieves?"

"You sound like that man who made such a commotion in the Temple the day before last," said Rebecca. "You'd better watch yourself."

"You saw him? That man, Jesus?" Binah hopped from her stool and grabbed Rebecca by the elbow. "Tell me."

"It's too dangerous." Rebecca spoke in a hushed voice below the din of the kitchen. "Roman soldiers and spies are everywhere. Even the Roman governor,

Pontius Pilate, has come to Jerusalem. They say he fears an uprising during the Passover festival."

"I've heard talk of Jesus," said Binah. "He dares to challenge the Sadducees and Pharisees. Now that you've seen him, you must tell me everything."

Rebecca sighed. "He turned over the tables of the money changers. He argued with the scribes, called the Pharisees hypocrites." Her hands worked faster, and she threw a nervous glance over her shoulder as she told what she had seen on an errand to the Temple.

"He spoke in stories, but it's clear what he means. There are those who appear righteous, but their hearts are filled with greed and self-importance."

"Does he say God will slay the powerful?" Binah interrupted. She pushed Rebecca aside. "You're so slow. We'll be here all night."

"No. He says forgive your enemies, be compassionate to all."

A shattering sound drowned Rebecca's words. The bowl Binah had started to scour lay in shards on the stone floor. Binah fell to her knees and scrambled to pick up the pieces, trying to fit them back together.

She jumped at the sound of the chief steward's voice. "What happened?"

"It was her." Binah pointed at Rebecca. "The new girl's a clumsy oaf."

"I'll deal with her," said the steward, frowning. "Go wait at the back gate. It's nearly midnight, and the wine for tomorrow has not arrived. Bring me word as soon as you see the wine merchant coming."

Not looking at Rebecca, Binah wiped her wet hands on her skirt and scurried away. Shouts erupted in the courtyard as she came up the flagstone steps from the kitchen.

A crowd of men had come through the gate: guards with torches, armed with swords and clubs. They led a bearded man, his hands tied behind his back. He must be a criminal, Binah thought, for they jeered at him and jerked him along. But the man did not struggle or flinch.

"You saved others, save yourself," one captor yelled at the man.

"Jesus, let's see a miracle," shouted another.

Binah's breath caught. It was him—Jesus of Nazareth. The jostling bunch came nearer, and she glimpsed his face in the flickering torchlight. His brown hair hung to his shoulders. He had the hands and shoulders of a man who worked hard.

After all she had heard about Jesus, she had expected someone more impressive. *He looks no different than any man in the village where I grew up.* About to turn away, she met his eyes.

The clamor of voices and stir of bodies faded. Held in his gaze, it was as if he and she stood there alone. His ragged breathing, the sweat on his brow, the trembling of his upper lip—all moved her with pity. Binah stepped from the shadows and reached a hand out to him.

But the guards pushed her back and swept the prisoner inside. Binah knew about the powerful men who were gathered upstairs. She shuddered at the thought of Jesus being dragged before them. What chance would this poor village man have? Following, she saw Jesus disappear with the guards behind heavy doors of polished Lebanon cedar. Pressing her ear to a crack, Binah heard only a murmur. She could do nothing for him here.

She raced back down to the courtyard. Where were the Nazarene's disciples? Surely someone could stand up with Jesus and argue in his behalf?

The night air was cold. A knot of soldiers had kindled a fire in the center of the yard and stood warming their hands around it. Among them, Binah spied a man dressed in the coarse tunic of a peasant. He was no guard. Could he be one of Jesus' friends?

Binah stepped closer but kept to the shadows. It wouldn't be proper for her to mingle with the men. Disgusted at the crude words she heard passed around the circle, she peered at the stranger. He didn't join in the joking, but when he did speak, Binah recognized his Galilean accent. Why was he standing here doing nothing while his master faced his interrogators alone?

"You are from Galilee," Binah burst out. "You were with Jesus."

The man darted a glance at her. "I don't know what you're talking about," he said. Immediately he turned and headed toward the gate. The other men laughed, and one of them reached for Binah, grabbing her skirt. Pulling away, she followed the retreating man. A rooster ran across her path, and she kicked at it, muttering. Where are the crowds who followed this Jesus?

Outside the gate Binah caught up to him. "You," she said, "you're one of his disciples."

"I do not know the man."

Binah clenched her fists and glared at him, but before she could say more the wine merchant's cart appeared. Not wanting to feel the back of the chief steward's hand, she ran to report the arrival.

Though the darkest part of the night had fallen, Binah and the other servants worked on. All cooking and cleaning needed to be finished before the Sabbath began the following sunset. Though she longed to steal away and find out what was happening to Jesus, Binah had no opportunity. When she dropped to her sleeping mat, exhausted, her last thoughts were of the man from Galilee.

The next morning the whole house buzzed with news. Soldiers had taken Jesus to the Roman palace. Pontius Pilate had sentenced him to die by crucifixion.

Binah gasped when she heard. "What's he done to deserve such a death?" she asked. No one had an answer, and there was little time to talk, what with the day's chores waiting.

Kneeling down before a huge tub, Binah scrubbed and wrung out laundry. She was glad to be out of the kitchen, to avoid facing Rebecca. But like every other task in the house, laundry seemed to have no end. As she worked, she thought of Jesus, going back over all she had heard about the man. He had performed miracles—healing lepers, making the blind see. Yet now he would die.

Or could he save himself? Hanging up the last silk gown to dry, Binah made up her mind to find out.

The noise and stench of the street flooded over her as she slipped between elbows and laden donkeys. So many pilgrims were in Jerusalem for the Passover, and it seemed all of them were out this morning. Roman soldiers were everywhere, their helmets shining in the sun.

Binah cut through narrow passageways to a spot where she knew the Romans would pass on their way to crucifying a prisoner. She'd wait there, on the route to Golgotha, the hill outside the city where people were hung on crosses to die.

Gasping for breath, and just in time, she squeezed

between several women in the crowd lining the road. A small procession approached. Bent low, Jesus carried a heavy wooden cross. Soldiers walked beside him, dragging two other prisoners. A centurion brought up the rear. The women around Binah began weeping.

A crown of thorns circled Jesus' head, sending rivulets of blood down his face. He stumbled under the weight of the cross, regained his footing, and went on. Binah could reach out and touch him if she dared. The scent of sweat and blood wafted to her nose and she swallowed hard, holding back her breakfast. The women around her beat their fists against their breasts, a stream of grief wailing out from under their veils.

Jesus halted. He was speaking. Binah leaned closer.

"Do not weep for me...." She strained to hear but couldn't catch any more. Then, once again, he looked into her eyes. A power coursed through her, blinding her for a moment, like sunlight reflecting off water.

And then she could see. Oh, how bitter her heart had become. She criticized her father, lorded over Rebecca, even lied to shift blame away from herself.

She watched Jesus struggle up the road until he and the cohort disappeared from sight. He would die this day, but Binah knew his spirit would not. It had kindled a spark in her, and she would nurture it. Like a flame travels a wick, this spark would seek its fuel and refuse to go out.

ABOUT THE STORY

In all four Gospels a servant girl confronts Peter, prompting the disciple's famous denial of Jesus. While powerful men question Jesus upstairs, below in the courtyard the lowly servant girl puts Peter on the spot. A young woman with no name, no means, and no religious authority or political power points to truth in this story. While the men above rejected the truth spoken by Jesus, the girl below persisted in seeking truth despite repeated lies.

Binah, whose name means "insight" in Hebrew, is one of countless unnamed women throughout history who has spoken truth despite her low status and the refusal of the culture to hear her voice.

M. C. F.

LOVE CASTS OUT FEAR

Early on the first day of the week, while it was still dark,
Mary Magdalene came to the tomb.
—Christian Bible, John 20:1

M ary Magdalene froze midstep in the dark street
and held her breath. There, it came again—the
sound of footsteps and the metallic clink of armor. She
darted into an archway, pressing back against the wall.

The sound of soldiers' sturdy steps moved closer.
She heard voices and the clang of sword and shield.

"I say, crucify a few more," said a harsh voice.
"That'll keep the riffraff in line."

"And make our job easier," answered another with
a laugh.

Mary Magdalene clenched her teeth to still her
trembling, grateful that the shadows had not yet given
up to the dawn.

The soldiers passed, their laughter rolling out
behind them.

Mary Magdalene didn't move. The pungent scent

of the spices she had packed into her basket drifted to her nose. The aloe for anointing the body, the myrrh— her eyes filled with tears. There would be a stench of decay now, on the third day.

"Oh, Jesus," she whispered. "How can I go on without you?" She choked back a sob. *Somehow I must.*

Pulling her woven cloak tightly around her, Mary Magdalene peered from the doorway where she huddled. Mary—the mother of James and Joseph—and Salome would be waiting. Swift, quiet steps brought her to the heavy wooden door. Her soft tap was answered, and she heard the bolt drawn back.

The two women slipped out, and the door was quickly locked again. Mary Magdalene embraced them.

"Is no one else coming?" asked Salome.

"None," said Mary Magdalene. "I told Peter, Matthew, and the others about the guard posted at the tomb. They begged me not to go. They're afraid all of us will be arrested." She looked from Salome's tear-blotched cheeks to Mary's wide eyes, and she squared her shoulders. "I have to go. I must see Jesus."

"Yes," whispered Salome. "Let's go."

They chose narrow back streets, wrapped in their cloaks, moving silently. Mary Magdalene's mind returned to images of Jesus hanging on the cross, his body broken and bloody. She shook her head, trying to clear away the memory, but she couldn't.

She had watched Joseph of Arimathaea and Nicodemus carry him to the tomb just before sundown and the start of the Sabbath. She could neither sleep nor eat in the night and day that followed, her chest aching, her stomach sick. When night came again to the locked room where she had hidden with a group from Galilee, she had made her decision. She couldn't hide herself like a rat in a hole, not after what Jesus had done for her.

Mary Magdalene remembered the day she'd met him. His gentle hands wiped blood from her face, his soft words soothed like a warm bath. He seemed to feel all her agony and did not cringe from it.

One of the demons had taken hold of her that morning. Her brother had bound her hands and feet for her own safety. But she'd broken free and run through the village, cursing, tearing at her hair and clothing. It had been the same as always. The demons gripping her like a prisoner, convulsing her body and torturing her mind. The children chasing her, pelting her with stones.

She'd crouched behind the well, clawing at her own skin. Then, just when she had risen up, ready to cast herself into the water, Jesus had appeared. Jesus—who made the blind see and the lame walk—had freed her. He'd driven seven demons from her body. He'd made her a new person.

But now he was gone.

Mary Magdalene stumbled. Her bare foot caught on a root branching out onto the steep path leading to the garden. She fell to her knees and groaned, rubbing her stinging toes. *If she could touch him, just be near him one more time and tell him all he had meant to her…*

Salome and the other Mary caught up with her.

"What about the stone?" asked Mary. "It's so huge. How will we move it?"

"Even the three of us will not have the strength," said Salome.

Mary Magdalene stood. "We can roll it away. Somehow we'll do it." She turned and the others followed her to the tomb.

Mary Magdalene steeled herself to face the guard. Surely he would see they meant no trouble. They had come only to anoint the body.

But no guard stopped them, and they walked right up to the tomb. In the dim light of dawn, the crypt appeared to be open. Mary Magdalene blinked her eyes. She looked again at the large stone. It rested aside from the hole in the craggy hill.

The other women gasped. Mary Magdalene fought for breath, her heart pounding like waves in a storm. They clutched each other, unmoving.

The first rays of sunrise stretched across the sky and touched the opening of the tomb. Clinging to one another, the women advanced, bending over to see inside. A cool draft played across their faces.

The tomb was empty.

"They've taken him," breathed Mary Magdalene. Her body felt hollow, like a shaft of wheat sucked empty by the desert sun.

The women backed out of the tomb. Without a word, Salome and Mary gathered their skirts and ran, heedless of the rocks and thorns. But Mary Magdalene stood weeping. She leaned against the limestone of the tomb, her cheek pressed against the veined rock, her tears flowing down it. She tried to remember the look of his face, the sound of his voice, but it was gone. Gone, like rain that passes in the heat of day, leaving no trace.

"Woman, why are you crying?" Mary Magdalene started at the sound of the voice. She turned around to look at the man standing there. Maybe he was the gardener. She swallowed and found her voice.

"Sir, if you have carried him away, tell me where you have put him."

"Mary." That one word floated to her ears, so familiar. Her heart leapt.

"*Rabboni?* Teacher?"

"Mary," he said again.

She ran several steps toward him, looking into those warm brown eyes with the same clear gaze, seeing every hair of his beard shining in the morning sun. All strength deserted her, and she slipped to her knees. Shaking like an olive leaf in a night breeze, she buried her face in her hands.

"Are you some demon come to torment me in my grief?" she cried.

"Mary, do not fear." Lifted as if by strong hands, she stood and reached toward him.

"Lord, it is you," she breathed. "I saw you die—I don't understand."

"Faith is required, not understanding. Go and tell my friends that I am alive." As he finished speaking, Jesus disappeared.

Mary Magdalene stared at the space where he had been, the grasses crushed where he had stood. A smile curved her lips and spread across her face. Light as the wind, she ran down the hill. She must tell Peter, James, and John the news. She had seen Jesus. He had spoken to her. Would they believe it? How could they? It seemed impossible. But she knew now that Jesus would be with her always.

ABOUT THE STORY

All four Gospel writers tell slightly different accounts of the death, burial, and resurrection of Jesus. But all agree Mary Magdalene is the primary witness to these essentials of the Christian faith. She is known as the Apostle to the Apostles.

This story borrows details from several of the different accounts. According to the Gospel of Mark (16:9), Jesus healed Mary Magdalene, driving out seven demons that possessed her. Mary became one of Jesus' most faithful followers, accompanying him throughout Galilee as he healed the sick and suffering and preached justice and love.

The realization that early Christians believed a woman, Mary Magdalene, was the first person to see Jesus after the Resurrection, opens the door to reading Scripture with a feminist eye. Once that door is opened, there is no going back.

M. C. F.

WEAVING A CHURCH

We sat down and spoke to the women who gather there. A certain woman named Lydia, a worshiper of God, was listening to us; she was from the city of Thyatira and a dealer in purple cloth. The Lord opened her heart to listen eagerly to what was said by Paul.
                    —*Christian Bible, Acts 16:13–14*

The dampened scarf that Lydia tied about her head kept her from perspiring in the late morning sun. Seated sidesaddle on her donkey, Lydia steadied a dripping basket of whelks against her hip. Fresh and salty from the sea, the snail-like creatures rocked forward and back with the animal's stride. The harbor of Neapolis on the Aegean Sea gleamed in turquoise tones behind her. With each step, the goat-trodden hills of Philippi loomed closer. A scent of olives hung in the air. *Sometimes those trees smell as rancid as my dyes,* she thought.

Lydia came to her mud-walled house and sunken-roofed dye sheds just outside the Roman city gates. Her place remained here near the putrid refuse dump because Philippians did not want to dwell in the stench of either.

An apprentice, Evodia, greeted her. She handed two scrolls with wax stamps to Lydia. "These came by courier. It looks like Paul's seal!"

"Already?" Lydia said, a touch of excitement in her voice.

Lifting the basket of whelks from the donkey's saddle with thick, sun-browned arms, Evodia said, "I'll begin cracking these. We have several orders to fill—another Roman wedding. All the women want purple cloth." Evodia rolled her eyes. "None of them has a measure of imagination."

"Evodia, we are blessed that these women still trade with us, in spite of their belief that our Christian faith defies Rome."

Lydia slipped off the donkey, stretching her arms and legs. "Is Syntyche here? Perhaps she can help you with the whelks."

"*Syntyche?*" Evodia said. "She says preparing slimy whelks is *beneath* her. Spinning, weaving, greeting customers, taking orders, and sorting fleeces is enough work."

"Evodia, that doesn't sound like our Syntyche," Lydia said gently. She thought, *The girls even argue over chores now, too. I hope Paul has some insight for me in handling their quarrels.*

Watching Evodia walk toward the shed, Lydia noticed the girl's garments. They were as stained with dye as her fingers. She looked down at her own dress—

a mostly brown sheep's wool, the wool least useful for coloring. *If only I could someday treat the girls or myself to a purple dress! Or even a yellow one, dyed with some of the weeds growing around here.*

Then Paul's words came to her: "How many artisans can afford their own work? The Holy Spirit nourishes us through the creation of that work. And this is why we can let it go—for a price that makes mockery of the hours of labor and skill." *The wisdom of a tent weaver,* she mused, patting her donkey's neck. *How I miss his counsel!*

With the scrolls in one hand, Lydia led the donkey to the water trough beneath a willow tree, a shady spot where she and her community often gathered to pray and break bread. She opened the letter from Paul addressed to her.

Dear Lydia,

Greetings. Thank you for your last letter and the cloth you have sent. It sold here for a fine price— Timothy and I shall eat and sleep well for weeks. You have worked with the zeal of athletes in building a Christian community in Philippi—ever as hard as you spin, weave, and dye your goods.

Lydia, your skills in cultivating solidarity is something I wish I had—it would make for better results here in Thessalonica. Trust in this gift from

God. I am quite certain that the One who began this good work in you will see that it is finished. While women have brought their sons to listen to our Gospel, my followers here do not show the strength of faith of my Philippian sisters and brothers in Christ.

I do hope to return to Philippi—perhaps on my way back to Ephesus. I thank my God whenever I think of you; and every time I pray for all of you, I pray with joy. When I come, I will finish making the tent you so thoughtfully agreed to leave on the loom until my return. I will take it with me to sell in Galatia or Cappadocia.

As for Evodia and Syntyche—please urge them not to quarrel. Our faith is not one of rules such as who may speak about the Lord. Only love matters. There should be no competition among you. Love is most important.

Your household, one that was formerly despised because of your profession, is now the center for new life in Philippi! Rejoice!

My lamp burns dim. May the grace and peace of God our Father and the Lord Jesus Christ be upon you.

Paul

I forgot to ask—who sent that sweet fragrance?

Lydia smiled at Paul's last question. *Syntyche must have included blossoms in the parcel,* Lydia thought. *How she hates to put them into vats of simmering water for dyes!*

Leaning against the willow, Lydia closed her eyes. Swallows chirped. For a few moments she imagined herself there again with Paul, Timothy, and Silas at the Roman garrison in Philippi on the night of the earthquake. The quake that had shaken the prison in which the men were held, where they had been singing praises to God. Lydia would never forget how the walls had crumbled to the foundation, throwing open cell doors and unleashing the trio's chains. And how she had said to Paul and the others, "When you are convinced that I believe in the Lord, come to my house and stay."

And it's been nothing but ridicule ever since, Lydia thought, frowning. The pagan Philippians had criticized her for housing the prisoners. "They are no better than soothsayers! Why would you risk worshiping just one god?"

Lydia opened her eyes. *This new faith of mine is not all sweetness and love. There's a certain amount of sting involved. The sting of keeping on—in times of doubt and of persecution by neighbors, when our own Christian community quarrels.... Perhaps I should counsel the girls today,* she thought, getting up.

The parched earth crunched beneath her sandals as she walked to the dye shed. The Roman aqueduct that carried water to the city cast a short shadow of itself on the ground.

Stepping under the trellis overgrown with hibiscus, she said to Evodia, "Paul wrote to say he will come to Philippi on his way home to Ephesus." The shade of the flowering vine helped to cool the workspace, where an open fire heated vats of indigo.

"Thank goodness," Evodia said, pinning up her hair with a comb. "I would like to talk with him about Syntyche. She thinks that since she was baptized nearly a year before me, she has contemplated Christ longer and therefore should be the one who prepares sermons."

The women stepped upwind of the rotten-smelling dye vessels.

"Evodia," Lydia said. "Perhaps I can help you see things differently. I will speak to Syntyche about helping you with the dyes. But remember that I asked her to greet customers because she speaks Greek, Latin, and Aramaic. She also knows her sums." Evodia didn't look at Lydia as she slipped several skeins of undyed thread into the indigo vat.

Taking Evodia's hands into her own, Lydia said, "Like preparing a sermon or leading a prayer, the work we do with our hands is also an offering."

Evodia nodded. "I understand what you mean, Lydia. I just don't know what's gotten into Syntyche," she said, adding dung chips to the flames beneath the whelk vat.

Lydia handed her a few more. "We must keep

working together, without quarreling. As Paul's letter said to me, we women struggle with 'the zeal of athletes' to strengthen God's church in Philippi." Evodia smiled. Lydia knew Paul's words would get through to her.

The women walked to the workbench where Evodia had cracked open dozens of whelks. Lydia and her apprentice scooped the shells into bowls, then poured them into the vat.

"Let's fill orders for the Romans—with gladness— knowing that as we do, we support ourselves and Paul's good works," Lydia said. "And let us find happiness in this lowly profession. We are cocreators with God, making beautiful dyes!"

"Like these blues," Evodia said, lifting a skein from the indigo vat and raising it into the air with a long-handled spoon. Lydia watched as the natural color of the yarn turned from yellow to green to blue, like a dawn sky changing from hue to hue. *Miraculous!* Lydia thought. Every time she witnessed this transformation when dyeing with whelks or indigo, she experienced a reunion with the divine, the "conversion of heart" about which Paul spoke.

"Lydia, perhaps the Roman women would like this dye lot for their wedding cloth."

"I'll send them samples. But first, I'd like to write back to Paul. Maybe I can catch the afternoon courier at the city gate."

Lydia went to her house. Inside, she reached across

her work table, stacked with cloth, clay tablets, and scrolls, for the walnut-shell ink and a fresh piece of parchment. She began her letter.

My Dearest Paul,
    Like a regenerative dye vat, your words, arriving in letters, strengthen our newly spun church...

ABOUT THE STORY

Lydia of Philippi lived about fifty years after Jesus' death. Philippi was a Roman colony in Macedonia, which is present-day Greece. The words that introduce this story are all that is written about Lydia. However, Paul's Letter to the Philippians speaks of the support he received from the community of Christians in Philippi—of which Lydia was his first convert. Perhaps he sent other letters to the Philippians, and even to Lydia herself.

Lydia's artistry offered her a unique perspective in understanding the fundamentals of her faith. Her role as a merchant and employer gave her the skills with which to organize a church, and she was blessed with a special gift for drawing people into her life. Christians are still doing what Lydia did with her gift in Philippi—building communities and congregations united in the love of God.

M. N. S.

MUSLIM
STORIES

THE NIGHT WIND

In the name of Allah, Most Gracious, Most Merciful:

To Allah belong the East and the West: whithersoever you turn, there is the Presence of Allah.
                                        —Qur'an 2:115 (The Heifer)

Eve stood tall, noble and beautiful as Adam, her mate. Hundreds of lovely tresses, studded with garnet gems and roses, formed her crown and rustled like the sound of leaves in a breeze. Eve's eyes were like clear, emerald pools of water. Her long, graceful fingers and wrists were adorned with pearls and opals. She was much like Adam in form, except that her skin was silken and her melodic voice rang with the laughter of birdsong.

Together they lived in the Garden, where they had neither hunger nor thirst, where it was neither too hot nor too cold. They had the blessed companionship of each other. The trees and bushes were laden with honey-sweet fruit perfectly ripened.

Allah taught Eve and Adam the names of all the animals, all the grasses, flowers and trees. These things were not taught to the angels made from light, nor to the jinns made from fire. Even though Allah fashioned humans from clay, they were to have certain knowledge above other beings. And because of this, Allah asked all the angels and jinns to bow down before Eve and Adam. All did so, all except for Iblis, Satan, the proudest jinn of them all. So the first sin belonged to Iblis: The first sin was pride.

> "We said: 'O Adam! You and your wife dwell in the Garden, and eat of the bountiful things therein as you will, but do not approach this tree, or you run into harm and transgression.'"—Qur'an, 2:35 (The Heifer)

And so Iblis hid in the Garden in the body of the most beautiful of creatures, in the form of a camel with a tail and mane the colors of rainbows, eyes like two shimmering planets, and an aroma of ambergris and musk.

When Iblis saw Eve and Adam, he fell to the ground, weeping and weeping before them, so that they both reached out to him in their grief and concern. "What makes you cry?" they asked.

Iblis spoke from the mouth of the camel, "I am crying because of you. You will die and be separated from this place. I am crying for you because you think this paradise will last forever."

And so Iblis tempted them to draw near to the tree of immortality and eat from the fruit that Allah had forbidden them. No sooner had they tasted of the fruit than the crowns flew off of their heads, the rings and pearls dropped off of their fingers, and their robes and clothes disappeared. And each article, as it departed, cried out, "We only clothe the obedient and humble servants of Allah."

Iblis had no remorse and so his legs drew into the cavity of his body. He was outcast from the Garden and forever condemned to squirm in the dust as a serpent, the eternal enemy of Eve and Adam.

But Eve and Adam begged Allah's forgiveness and thus were pardoned, but still punished. They too were outcast from the Garden, yet they were promised timeless guidance from Allah to relieve their suffering.

"We said: 'Get you down all from here; and if, as is sure, there comes to you guidance from Me, whosoever follows My guidance, on them shall be no fear, nor shall they grieve.'"—Qur'an 2:38 (The Heifer)

Eve woke to an empty blue sky and a cold, thin wind. Her lips felt dry; she didn't know the word for this feeling—she had never experienced it. She touched them. They felt rough, like an animal's snout. Underneath her head, her back, her legs, she sensed uneven, rocky ground. This too was new, this dull pain. *Where am I? Where is Adam?* She spoke these words aloud: "Where am I? Where is Adam?" She shouted them, this time to the sky.

The wind never answered. Eve sat up. She saw that she was on a mountaintop. Pink and orange hills, dry and buckling, ringed her perch. In every direction barren crevices sliced the steep mountainside.

Standing up, Eve felt closer to the ground, naked, no longer so tall. Her hands reached for her tresses, finding them dusty and matted. Her bare feet found no soft surface on which to rest.

Eve began to weep. Hiding her face in her palms, she dropped to her knees and sobbed, the thirsty ground soaking up her tears. After a time, exhausted, she lay on her back again and gazed up at the sky. Melting like hot gold, the sun seemed to be abandoning her too. Eve watched the sky empty of light, not knowing what would happen next.

When the sky filled with innumerable, dazzling, small silver suns, Eve knew Allah's presence was still with her. The slightest breeze caressed her and told her it was so. And something else curled by and through her all night: a thin ribbon of Adam's voice, from the west. *Where is Eve, where is Eve?* The wind lifted Adam's voice to Eve and Eve's to Adam, and each thought that the other was close by, although between them were countless lands.

Softness surrounded her, cloudlike. In her dream, the heavy air of the Garden, rich and infused with nectar, brought her to waking. She found herself on a thick bed of herbs and flowers, green and lush wherever her tears had spilled. Burying her face in it, feeling the velvet petals and pollen between her fingers, she laughed. More tears welled up and fell, joyous and sad at once, relief and longing loosening the knot in her chest.

Eve could name the things surrounding her: crocus, aster, lily, ginger, anise, and poppy. She spoke their names and wept. As she did, the green spread across and down the mountainside, carpeting the direction from which she had heard Adam's voice. Eve stood and began to walk west. And she called to her companion, "Adam, I am coming!"

For a hundred years Eve wept and walked, following the sun westward, the world behind her watered to life by tears, a groundswell of birdsong, cicadas, and crickets filling the valleys as she departed. At night, the voice of Adam sang to her across the stars. Each evening the wind blew warmer and sweeter, and so she knew Allah brought them closer to each other and that her punishment was nearly over.

When Eve reached the sea, she didn't know what to do. Again she wept for her companion, and each tear that fell into the sea transformed into a pearl. But the wind increased, the waves made great roaring curls, and the trees shook and clattered. Then the angel Michael appeared to her and said, "God has accepted Adam's repentance and your repentance and blesses you both. Take these garments and enter the Sanctuary." The angel of Allah gave her a chemise and veil. He then guided her to enter Mecca from the east.

"O you Children of Adam! We have bestowed raiment upon you to cover your shame, as well as to be an adornment to you. But the raiment of righteousness—that is the best."—Qur'an 7:26 (The Heights)

"Praise be to Allah, most merciful and compassionate!" she cried as she entered Mecca.

And Jabal-e-rahmah, the Mountain of Mercy, replied, "Welcome!"

Eve climbed the mountain and waited for seven days. When she saw birds, grasses, and trees spreading toward her from the west, from the tears of Adam, she knew her beloved was close by.

So Eve saw Adam enter Mecca from the west, praising Allah as the angels did: "Here am I. Here am I," shouted Adam. "Praise, glory, and the kingdom are Thine. Here am I." Adam cried to Allah, and the angel Gabriel commanded him to go seven times around the holy place. These are the sanctifying things that all pilgrims to Mecca repeat to this very day.

And before Eve embraced Adam atop the Mountain of Mercy, Eve bathed and purified herself in the well water of Zamzam to remind herself again of God. The water was cold and sweet and rich with perfumes of the Garden. Eve bathed in it, and from her tresses the earth was eternally infused with the aroma of flowers.

ABOUT THE STORY

The story of Eve and Adam first appeared in Hebrew Scripture, long before the Qur'an was recorded. The Qur'an provides a slight contrast to the story of Eve as told in Genesis: In the Qur'an, Eve and Adam are tempted at the same time. They then are quickly forced to leave the Garden of Paradise, along with the serpent. Although the Qur'an does not separate the couple on earth for a time of repentance, the stories told in the Islamic tradition. do.

This story of the first woman and her mate is greatly expanded from the simple account found in the Qur'an, where Eve is called Hawa. It is woven together with a collection of historical and modern storytelling versions. For example, the authoritative Qur'anic historian Al-Tabari (900 C.E.) is used as the source for the jinn Iblis's trickery. In Islam there are said to be three types of beings: angels, jinns, and humans. Angels, made from light, always follow Allah's guidance; jinns, made from fire, can stray from righteousness; humans, made from clay, have an element of free will in deciding whether or not to follow Allah's guidance. The Muslim storyteller Al-Kisa'i (1200 C.E.), in his poetic and entrancing stories, inspired the elements of this story: the character of Eve, the beautiful camel forever transformed into a serpent, the life-giving trail of tears, and the pilgrimage to Mecca for humanity's sanctification.

There is indeed a Mount Mercy in Mecca, with a small mosque at its summit. Pilgrims still go there to honor the first union of Adam and Eve on earth.

S. C.

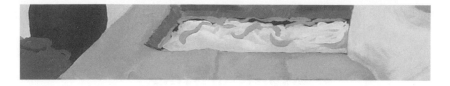

THE WATERS OF ZAMZAM

In the Name of Allah, Most Gracious, Most Merciful:

*Don't you see that Allah sends down water from the sky,
and forthwith the earth becomes clothed with green?*
— *Qur'an 22:63 (The Pilgrimage)*

In the darkness of her tent, Hagar lay on her mat singing a gentle lullaby to her child, Ishmael, who suckled at her breast. Exhausted from her day of labor— she had carried water to and from the well many times that day—she drifted into sleep.

"Hagar! Arise!" A sudden shouting awoke her from a dream state. "Hagar!"

The voice sounded like Abraham. *But why would he be coming to me shouting in the night?* She heard the approach of heavy footsteps.

"Husband, is that you?" she called, rising to look outside. Ishmael began to fuss in her arms. "*Shh,* little one—it's only your father coming. No need to cry."

Abraham appeared in the doorway of her tent. "Prepare yourself and Ishmael." He told her. "We must leave tonight."

"Leave? Why, Abraham?"

"Come quickly, Hagar."

"But where are we going?" Hagar questioned her husband as she gathered a few possessions: blankets, a cooking pot, her jewelry. The baby continued to cry. "*Shh,* Ishmael, you must not cry." She tried to comfort her child but the words caught in her throat.

"There is no need to pack your belongings, Hagar. Allah will provide for the journey."

Hagar was accustomed to the nomadic life: packing and unpacking, moving with the seasons, taking the flocks to the best grazing land. But to leave in the middle of the night, just the three of them? It was incomprehensible.

"Abraham, please tell me—where are you taking your wife and only child in the night?" Abraham stood just outside the tent, waiting for her, a darkened silhouette against the starlit sky.

"We'll know our destination at the end of the journey," he replied. "Come quickly—we must leave at once."

Carrying Ishmael in a sling across her shoulder, Hagar reluctantly fell in step behind Abraham. Single file, they passed out of the camp, beyond the tents, beyond the goats and sheep grazing on the hillside. Abraham carried a water skin and a leather satchel filled with dates and dried meat. Ishmael, calmed by the sway of his mother's step, fell back to sleep.

For several days they traveled, walking through the cool nights and early mornings, then resting in whatever shade they could find during the scorching heat of the day. Abraham seemed distant, as if engaged in some inner dialogue.

"Where are we going? How will this end?" Hagar asked these questions over and again without receiving an answer. Eventually she kept silent and busied herself protecting Ishmael from the heat and blowing sand. *As long as we are together,* she told herself, *we will be safe.* In the afternoon of the fifth day, the family arrived in a barren valley, a wide expanse between two low hillsides. Hagar looked around; she had never seen a place so desolate as this. There was no sign of water. There were no signs of life. It had been days since Hagar had seen a lizard or even a bird.

"This is the loneliest place on the earth," she said.

"This is the *holiest* place on earth," replied Abraham as he lifted the water skin and satchel of food from his shoulder. Hagar took Ishmael from his sling and sat down on the hot sand, preparing to suckle him. As she did, Abraham placed the water and the remaining provisions on the ground beside her. Looking deeply into her eyes he said, "Allah will provide for you here." Before Hagar could find words to speak, Abraham stroked Ishmael's flushed cheek and said, "Farewell, Hagar." Then he turned and started walking in the direction they had just come.

"Abraham!" she called out. "Where are you going?" She waited for him to stop, to explain himself, to return to her. But Abraham continued walking.

"Abraham!" Her panic rose into her throat. "Come back!"

Hagar stood up and, carrying Ishmael, she ran after her husband, shrieking. "Is it the will of Sarah, your other wife, that you follow?" Abraham continued to walk. He did not look back.

"Abraham!" She shouted his name over and again, as she ran. "Abraham! If you are leaving me because my breath stinks or because I am not beautiful, then that makes me angry. But if this is part of Allah's wisdom for us, then I will submit."

As she finished speaking Abraham finally paused. He turned to his wife and said, his voice trembling, "Indeed, it is the will of Allah that you and Ishmael should stay here." And then Abraham turned again and began his journey home.

Alone with Ishmael, Hagar cast her gaze around the place, surveying the emptiness. The glaring sun cast a long shadow—the silhouette of a lone woman holding a child against the barren sand. Taking a deep breath, she said to her son, "God will not neglect us."

Days passed. Hagar drank the last of the water. No caravans passed within her sight. No clouds gathered overhead. Her thirst became an agony, and she no longer had milk for Ishmael. The child grew weak. His cheeks were flushed from the heat and his body lethargic. *I must find water. Must find something or someone to help us.*

Hagar placed Ishmael in a shallow gully where there was a small spot of shade, and then she ran to the top of the nearby hill. She scanned the horizon but saw nothing. She turned and began her way down the hill, past the rocky depression where Ishmael lay hidden, and then she continued on up the next hill. She reached the top, but again she saw nothing. Determined to find help, she ran back and forth between the two hilltops. She ran as if in a trance, searching but not seeing.

Scan the horizon. Squint into the eastern sun. I see no caravan line, no tents, no green oasis. Only wind and dust and fear. Find water. Keep searching.

Look up, look down, all around. Search the ground, even the dirt. Allah makes miracles.

Back down the hill. The way is steep, knees aching. Keep going, keep looking.

Another hillside. Run up. Breath stabs my chest like a dagger. Scorching hot sand. Reach the top. Scan the horizon. Nothing. Cannot give up. Must survive.

Seven times, Hagar ran between the hilltops. Exhausted and delirious with thirst, she came to the place where she had left Ishmael. She knelt on the ground and cradled his limp body.

130

"Allah!" she called out, her voice barely a whisper. "Why delay our salvation?" Overcome with thirst, Hagar lay down on the ground, her body curled around Ishmael.

Just as she slipped into sleep, Hagar felt Ishmael trembling in her arms. Like slow thunder, the ground around her began to rumble and shake. It seemed as if the earth would split apart. The baby was beating his arms and legs against the ground. "Ishmael," she cried, trying to soothe him. "Ishmael. I am here." But Ishmael's wild movements continued. Helpless to save herself or her child, Hagar cried out, "Allah! There is no God but you."

And just as Hagar spoke these words, Ishmael kicked the ground with his heel, sending forth a sudden geyser of clear, cool water.

"Water! Look, Ishmael. Allah has made this miracle for us!" Crystal clear water bubbled out of the ground, flooding the place where they lay.

Ecstatic, Hagar scooped her son up out of the spray, twirling him around in delight. "Thanks be to Allah!" she sang. Ishmael, suddenly revived, smiled and laughed, grasping at the dancing water. Droplets shone like fragments of light.

Before she drank, Hagar took up a sharp stone and dug out a deep basin around the spring, so the water would be contained and not run out across the sand.

She sat down to rest while the pool filled, and then she drank.

In time, grasses and shrubs grew in the place. A white-winged raven built its nest, and animals came to drink: rodents, lizards, gazelle, and leopards. One day, some travelers passing through were surprised to see a raven flying in the valley that had always been barren. They followed its flight and so they came to find the new spring.

Hagar heard the caravan approaching and, glad for the company of others, she went out to greet the travelers. "Welcome to Zamzam," she said, towering above them, tall and straight like a palm. "May Allah be with you."

"We are amazed to find water here, in this desert," they told her.

"There will always be water for those who come," Hagar replied with a generous smile. And she filled their vessels with water from the spring.

ABOUT THE STORY

Hagar and Ishmael settled at the spring of Zamzam where, according to Islamic tradition, their descendants flourished and gave rise to the Arab people. In this way Hagar links the Prophet Muhammad, peace be upon him, and thus all of Islam to the patriarch Abraham, who is remembered by Muslims, Jews, and Christians alike for his unique vision of an all-powerful yet merciful God. The Zamzam spring, which is located in Saudi Arabia in the city of Mecca, continues to play an important role in Islamic tradition. Every year, several million Muslims from around the world make the hajj, or pilgrimage to Mecca, the site of the Ka'ba, Islam's holiest shrine. As part of the hajj ritual, pilgrims retrace Hagar's steps, walking seven times between the two low-lying hills of Marwa and Safa, a total distance of approximately two miles. In addition, during the ritual they receive water that comes from the Zamzam spring, which continues to flow in the Great Mosque at the site of the Ka'ba.

Readers familiar with the biblical story of Hagar, described in the Book of Genesis, will find many similarities as well as some interesting differences. The story "A Thousand Wrinkles," which appears in the Jewish section of this book, tells a similar tale from the biblical Sarah's point of view. Each tale is told within its own tradition. "The Waters of Zamzam" used only Islamic source materials, while "A Thousand Wrinkles" relied on details found only in Jewish sources.

B. W.

A FAITH BLOSSOMS

In the name of Allah, Most Gracious, Most Merciful:

And thou hadst not expected that the Book would be sent to thee except as a Mercy from thy Lord...invite men to thy Lord.

—Qur'an 28:86–87 (The Narration)

K hadija's eyes flew open as her husband, Muhammad, jolted in his sleep. He had kicked off the covers, and his body glistened with sweat. Khadija looked out through the bedroom windows to the garden. Palm leaves painted a mosaic against the dawn. *Most Gracious, Most Merciful One, let him rest peacefully,* she prayed, stroking his thick, dark hair. *His calling tests him so.*

Slipping out of bed and into cool, cotton garments and her sandals, she hurried down the breezeway. The Prophet Muhammad's servant who had promised to accompany her and her maids to Mount Hira awaited her at the fountain in the courtyard. Even though Ramadan, the holy month of prayer, was over, Khadija felt the need to get away from the bustle of Mecca. She was tired of the endless haggling over prices with the caravan traders, the excuses for late merchandise, the troubles regarding sick pack animals. She thought that if she could clear her mind, she would make better decisions. A morning on the mountain above the city would offer her a chance to revive herself. And Khadija wanted to revisit the place where the Angel Gabriel had greeted Muhammad, to experience this gift in her own way, to contemplate what Muhammad had revealed to her.

Khadija stopped midway up Mount Hira to gaze at the isolated mountains all around. They cropped up here and there like impudent, humpbacked camels who, having folded their legs beneath them, refused to press onward through the sea of parched brown sand. Tucked between the hilly lumps of their hooves and knees and rumps were clusters of clay homes. In the middle of it all was the Ka'ba, the holy building about which the people of Mecca circled, inscribing in the cracked soil their prayers to the many gods. The cube-shaped shrine drew thousands of pilgrims to her city, and they in turn allowed her own business to prosper.

With each of Khadija's steps, the sounds of the market city diminished, replaced by the occasional tinkling of goat's bells. Taking a deep breath to slow her pulse from the climb, she said to her servants, "This is far enough. I will not go to the cave where the Prophet prays. Would you please leave me alone here for a while?"

"We'll set up our canopy on the other side of that outcropping," Muhammad's servant said, pointing west. "Simply wave your arms if you need anything."

One of Khadija's maids, Samiya, said, "I packed figs and bread for when you are hungry."

"You spoil me," Khadija said, sitting on a boulder. "I am in need of nothing as yet."

As the servants continued on, Khadija watched Samiya pull her spindle and a handful of wool from her satchel. Khadija called to her, "I invited you along today so that you would not have to work, yet you brought your spinning! Give that to me and rest. I insist."

"You are too kind," the young woman said, returning to give the wooden tool and soft fleece to Khadija.

Holding the end of the spindle in one hand, Khadija tapped it on her other palm. The whorl, splintered from use, scratched her skin. She examined it for a minute, taking in its nicks, and then looked out over the city of Mecca. By now, her merchants would have finished sweeping their stalls in the bazaar and displayed their goods from Syria—cloth, spices, carpets. She hoped that Muhammad could settle the accounting bill with one merchant in particular—an old dispute for which she'd lost patience.

A puff of wind carried the scent of sage and the last clink and clank of a flock as it disappeared over the shoulder of the mountain with a shepherd. Silence followed, though Khadija's ears still rang with the clamor of the market.

She scanned the ground, finding sage growing in the gravelly earth. Beside her left foot a crocus bloomed purple. *How it survives in this dry soil seems a miracle,* she mused. Then she thought, *I've never made time to think about this before—that a flower can grow in a desert. How could I have taken this for granted?*

Khadija removed her headscarf and shook her hair loose. With very little gray for her fifty-five years, her dark strands absorbed the heat of the sun, which felt soothing on her scalp. She began to weave the strands into a braid. The tightness in her neck relaxed as she worked, and new sounds crept into her consciousness: the buzz of a fly, the crinkle of a leaf disturbed by a lizard, the clatter of a stone slipping downhill. *Allah's signs. Small yet clear. Beautiful and abundant.* Oddly, she felt in good company in her aloneness. *No wonder Muhammad does not mind coming up here for days at a time,* she thought. *You need only turn your attention to God and you will find the Spirit everywhere.*

Thinking of Muhammad made her smile. She recalled the day when she first saw him. She had overheard him in the market saying to a dishonest spice merchant, "Give full measure when you measure, and weigh with even scales. That is better and fairer in the end." She had learned more about Muhammad's trustworthiness from the bearded men at the bazaar as they unwrapped their gold jewelry, copper pots, and earthenware for her to consider. She had learned also of his exceptional trading skills. For these reasons, she later told her caravan agents, she must hire him. But sitting in the shade of her terraced garden, where water trickled over and down the grooves carved into each step, she had told her women friends of another reason for hiring Muhammad: the walnut sheen of his hair.

Even now, a man of forty years, he still thrives among the shrewd caravan traders. Every bit the strong, young man I proposed to. She liked to tease Muhammad about this detail of their courtship, as she had done just last night. She had reminded him how she, with a little help from a matchmaker, had invited Muhammad to her house after the cooks had slaughtered a sheep. How her maids sent for her uncles to be witnesses and then invited her father to join in the feast. And long into the night, amid all the merriment, Khadija urged her father to marry her to Muhammad.

Imitating for Muhammad her father's disbelief, she had said, "And my father saying the next morning after he awoke, 'I have not married you to Muhammad. Why would I do this when the greatest men in Mecca have asked for you and I have not agreed?'"

Taking Muhammad's hands in hers, she had continued, "And my telling him, 'Because the greatest men of Mecca speak more highly of Muhammad than of one another.'"

Khadija grinned, as Muhammad had last night. Twirling the spindle against her thigh, she thought, *He will make a strong Prophet. He has gained many Meccans' respect, along with that of nearly everyone from here to Syria with whom he has traded on my caravan routes.*

Who could not see his wisdom? He among all the men I know has looked after the women and children of this tribe. He has spoken against those who divorce their wives when the women are still nursing their babies...urged our people not to smother their newborn girls in the sand from fear of want. Allah will provide, he assures them.

Khadija placed the spindle on the ground and picked up a pebble—dark black, like the sacred rock the Meccans revered in the Ka'ba. The Black Stone, believed to have fallen from the heavens. While Khadija respected this custom with which she had been raised, she embraced the Oneness of Allah that Muhammad proclaimed, the God of whom the Angel Gabriel spoke. She wanted to support her husband in his calling. Give back to him as he had given so much of himself to her.

The sun stood directly overhead. Noticing this, she felt something nagging her to go home, as if an invisible market hourglass lured her back to town, to opportunities that surely awaited her there. But Khadija wasn't ready to go. Some other presence willed her to stay.

Asked her to forget about finding the next customer or seeking the next coin.

Replacing her headscarf she knelt on the ground and scooped up sand in both hands, copying what Muhammad had shown her, ritual ablution to purify oneself before prayer. The Angel Gabriel had instructed Muhammad using water from a miraculous fountain that had gushed forth in a valley near this very same mountain. With the sand, since there was no water, Khadija cleansed her feet and hands and face. As she did this, it occurred to her that each stage of Muhammad's life seemed to have prepared him for what was to come, and for his role as a Prophet: He was first taken in by bedouins who had provided him with a healthier life in the desert. Then, orphaned around the age of seven, he had been raised by a trusted uncle. When he turned twenty-five, she, Khadija—a wealthy widow, fifteen years older than Muhammad—had married him. And now he was free to meditate for many days during Ramadan without worry that their trading would fall short.

The dry earth that collected in the soft spots between Khadija's fingers and toes robbed them of their moisture. A grain of dust blew into her eye, causing a tear. The wisp of wind carried the question, "Hasn't the hand of God always supported Muhammad?"

That afternoon, plunging into the throng of people and the pungent mix of dung and sun-dried olives smashed on the packed ground in the market, Khadija pulled her head covering over her face to stave off the smell. She spotted Muhammad's curls beneath his kaffiyeh among the other men on the corner where the carpet merchants sold their wares. He stood with a parchment in his hand, poring over figures. When he caught a glimpse of her, Muhammad flashed Khadija the wide smile that had won her some fifteen years ago. Then he rolled up his ledger as if nothing but his wife mattered to him.

Touching his arm, Khadija said, "Come, I have something to tell you."

Muhammad reached for a sprig of jessamine as a young vendor wheeled a cart with some of the flowers past the two of them. Tossing the boy a coin with one hand, he handed the fragrant bouquet to Khadija with the other.

"Muhammad," Khadija said, "I would like to pray with you, in the manner Gabriel taught, outside the Ka'ba. I want to support you the best way I can, as you lead our people in prayer. You are the Prophet chosen by God."

Muhammad's smile faded. A look of concern crossed his tanned face.

"I know," Khadija said. "Perhaps my actions will endanger my reputation among the merchants—but they might also follow my example."

"Khadija," Muhammad said gently.

"I insist. *Allah will provide,* Muhammad. I learned this in my prayers. God will help those of us who follow you."

She buried her face in the jessamine's white petals and inhaled deeply. Instead of its sweet fragrance, she smelled the tang of sage. Saw the purple bloom of a crocus. Felt comforted by another presence.

ABOUT THE STORY

Khadija was the first wife of the Prophet Muhammad, peace be upon him, and his only spouse until after her death. Both ancient and modern biographers of Muhammad agree that Khadija's devotion helped him proceed with his prophetic call to Islam.

This fictional story draws from varied accounts of Khadija's marriage and tries to follow what the biographer Ibn Ishaq wrote: "Allah preserve me from attributing to the Apostle words which he did not use." Some of Khadija's thoughts on Muhammad's wisdom or Muhammad's dialogue, such as "weigh with even scales," are borrowed from the Qur'an. Because Muslims believe that no one should speak for the Prophet, in this story he says little—but the story brings to life Khadija's and Muhammad's love and respect for each other.

M. N. S.

PRAYERS
IN THE DARKNESS

In the Name of Allah, Most Gracious, Most Merciful:

Seek Allah's help with patient perseverance and prayer: It is indeed hard, except to those who bring a humble spirit.
                    —Qur'an 2:45 (The Heifer)

M other! Look what a stranger gave us!" exclaimed Hasan.

Fatima, daughter of the Prophet Muhammad, finished wiping the face of her infant before looking up at the commotion. Hasan, her eldest son, stood grinning and breathless in the rough-hewn door frame, a plump hen tucked in his arm.

Husayn—just a year younger than his brother but a good deal smaller in size—and his little sister, Zaynab, scrambled from their seated positions on the floor, knocking over earthenware cups in the process.

"Mother, it's a really huge, fat chicken!" said Zaynab as she approached the frightened bird bundled in her brother's arms. "We haven't had meat in weeks! Can we cook it now? Can we?" she asked.

What Husayn lacked in stature he made up for in spunk; immediately, he closed in on the bird, trying to wrest it from his brother. "I want to hold it, Hasan! It's my turn!" The hen eyed them both nervously and tried to wing an escape.

Fatima hurried over to the struggling boys. "Easy now, we want to keep her nice and fat," she said in her most soothing voice. Still cradling the baby, Kulthum, in one arm, Fatima stroked the bird, examining it thoughtfully. Although calloused from the daily grinding of wheat, her hand sensed the bird's trembling body under its stiff feathers.

"Hasan, where did the hen come from?"

"A group of men just arrived at Grandfather Muhammad's house, Mother," he explained. "They said there was a battle in a village nearby, but we won, and now there are many things to share: camels, chickens, gold, and servants. One man even showed me a jeweled sword!"

Husayn's and Zaynab's eyes widened with each new detail. They were too young to go straight over to their grandfather's without permission, but never having seen the rewards of battle before, the two squirmed with anticipation.

"And the men have all gathered at Grandfather's house?" Fatima asked. "With all of these riches?"

"Well, some of the men have gone there, by the mosque. That's where one man recognized me as the Prophet's grandson and gave me this chicken."

"Oh, Mother!" burst Husayn. "Can't we go over and see? Can't I go back with Hasan?" Zaynab frowned at her brother.

Fatima stood in the dim light of her small, mud-walled home. She surveyed the sum of her possessions with an easy sweep of the eyes: a few cooking pots, some stones for grinding grain, a table, a velvet blanket, and a single leather cushion. By the door hung the camel skin, used during the day for carrying animal fodder, upon which she, her husband, and the children slept at night.

The possibility that her life could be lightened a bit by the spoils of battle made its way into her thoughts. She had no servants. She had married Ali, one of the Prophet's first converts to Islam. Like the Prophet, she and Ali lived a simple life.

"Hasan," Fatima suggested, "run over to Grandfather's house and tell Grandmother we have dinner for them tonight."

All three children looked crestfallen. Shoulders drooped, eyes fixed upon the floor—the silence grew loud. "But Mother," Husayn stammered at last, "we want some meat, too! We hardly ever get meat!"

Fatima steadied her youngest boy's chin between thumb and forefinger. "Have we ever gone hungry for long?" she asked.

He shook his head from side to side. "No, not for long."

"And when we are generous to others, how does Allah treat us?"

"Allah is always generous and compassionate, Mother."

"Good boy! Now, Hasan, go and do as I have asked. I also want you to whisper in Grandfather's ear that if someone is giving away servants, I could certainly use one." Fatima cringed just a bit after saying that, knowing her father might see it as greedy. But she couldn't help it. *I'm not asking for gold,* she told herself, *just help with the work of keeping my family fed.* She could grow a bigger garden. She could store more grain. There would be fewer bouts of hunger.

"Go now. Run and tell your grandfather we have something special for him. Husayn, you can go with your brother, but make sure you don't get in the way of the men."

Tears welled in Zaynab's eyes. She stared at her mother hopefully. Fatima held Hasan's forearm, restraining him from leaving. "Hasan, give Zaynab your treasure to hold." Obediently, he guided Zaynab's arms around the chicken, until she had a secure hold on it.

Fatima resumed her work. Though it was a hot autumn midafternoon, Fatima's home was just cool enough to feel comfortable.

Zaynab, studying the bird wrapped in her arms, interrupted her mother's thoughts. "Mother, do others get chicken for dinner every night?"

Fatima looked at her daughter out of the corner of her eye while continuing her cleaning. Even though the girl dressed in fabric as plain as the mud and straw walls of the house, Zaynab was a beauty—olive eyes contrasted with a fine complexion. Fatima sighed to herself, knowing that differences in wealth were probably too difficult for her young daughter to understand.

"Yes," Fatima replied. "Some probably do eat meat and dates and figs and bread almost every day. And perhaps they even eat until their stomachs insist that they stop!" She smiled. "But remember what we have each day. Tell me, my little gem, what nourishment of the *spirit* do we get every day?"

Zaynab had heard this line of reasoning many times before. She looked at her mother. "We get to live close to *Rasul* Allah—God's messenger. We get to be with the Prophet Muhammad every day."

Fatima walked across the room and leaned into her daughter's face, until they were nearly nose-to-nose. "That's right, my little pearl," teased Fatima, and they both chanted in unison, "Meat and sweets fill the stomach, but leave the soul hungry; words of the spirit are a feast everlasting." They giggled.

With the baby perched on her hip, Fatima put more kindling on the fire to refresh the embers. She grabbed the water skin, filled her cooking pot with water, and placed it over the fire. When it came to a rolling boil it would be just right for scalding the chicken—only then could the bird be easily plucked.

"I'll trade you one fat chicken for one fat baby!" Fatima teased as they swapped. Fatima took the chicken out back to the small, shaded courtyard. Zaynab followed, laying the baby against her shoulder.

Soon after, the boys reappeared, breathless, in the courtyard. "Grandfather was not at home," said the younger boy, "but Grandmother Aisha says she will cook tonight. Grandmother says you will always be Umm Abii-haa, your father's mother, if you continue to spoil Grandfather so much," Husayn grinned.

They chuckled at the pet name Fatima had been given by the community long ago. She had been called Umm Abii-haa soon after her mother, Khadija, died. She had tried to look after her father's every need since then—it was true. He, in turn, had attempted to make her the happiest girl on earth, to make up in some way for her loss.

The Prophet's second wife, Aisha, teased them both, saying that they looked, spoke, and acted so much alike that even their shadows got confused. If the Prophet was given a present, he insisted a portion go to Fatima. If Fatima was blessed with a gift, she felt incomplete unless she shared it with her father.

"Hasan, did you tell your grandmother we could surely use even one kitchen girl?" asked Fatima.

"Yes, Mother."

They heard the sound of boiling water splashing and sputtering the fire. "Ah, it grows late, my children! We must say a little prayer of thanks and get on with the business at hand, or there'll be no dinner for anyone!" She clasped the hen by its legs and let it rotate gently upside down. Hasan helped hold the bird still while Fatima slit its throat. Zaynab and Husayn stood a short distance away, transfixed. Mother and son were an efficient team, and before long the chicken was plucked, cleaned, and placed in the stew pot.

The smells of coriander, cumin, and garlic filled the house as the sunset warmed the city with its pink glow. Even though there was still much work ahead, this was Fatima's favorite time of day. Her baby nestled in the corner sleeping; the older children dashed in and out of the house, in and out of the courtyard, collecting treasures of pebbles and feathers. Soon the evening call to prayer would be sung from the mosque rooftop, and her father would lead the people in prayer.

Ali returned home after evening prayers and added a few onions to the stew pot. Goat cheese made from the Prophet's nanny goat topped off the bowls. Every morsel was complimented and savored while the boys recounted to their father the spoils of war—prize camels, saddles, and weapons.

"I have asked Father for just a little of it," confessed Fatima during one of the few pauses in conversation.

"A camel?" asked Ali, eyes twinkling. Fatima knew he was teasing.

"No, no. I requested some help for the house...if there is excess. It would allow me to do so much more for our family."

Ali responded with a brief nod of his head. The boys continued their story.

A few hours later, the whole family lay together on the camel skin. Kulthum snuggled between her parents on one side; the older children vied for a share of velvet blanket on the other.

An hour after falling asleep, Fatima felt a cool

pressure on her shoulder that slowly roused her. She opened her eyes. It was dark, but after a few moments she could sense, more than see, that her father, the Prophet Muhammad, leaned over her.

"Father, what is it?" Fatima asked. "What is wrong?" Ali, now also awake, started to get up.

"Keep your places," said the Prophet, his tone gentle, but serious. After a long pause he continued: "Shall I tell you a thing that is better than what you asked for?"

Fatima anticipated what was to come—she knew her father well. "Yes, Father," she replied obediently.

"Instead of the riches you have asked for, when you return to bed say, '*Allahu Akbar*—Allah is Great' thirty-four times. Then recite, 'All praises are for Allah' thirty-three times. And lastly, 'Glory to Allah' thirty-three times."

Fatima relaxed and let his message sink in. She never ceased to be surprised at the effect of her father's words. This time, they swept away the greedy knot that had gnawed at her stomach all day.

The Prophet said no more, but neither did he leave. Fatima began, in a quiet singsong, the recitation as he had instructed. Her voice found the melody in the prayer, the way that sacred Arabic moves like a stream rushing and pooling around boulders as it descends from the high mountains.

When she finished, Fatima felt cleansed, as if she'd been walking through those mountains, alongside that stream, in their brighter light.

ABOUT THE STORY

Fatima, the youngest of the four daughters of the Prophet Muhammad, peace be upon him, by his first wife, Khadija, is an intriguing character. Positioned between two powerful religious leaders—the Prophet Muhammad and one of his first converts to Islam, Ali—Fatima must have found her challenges with difficult living conditions to be at times both physical as well as spiritual.

A Hadith (saying and action of the Prophet) recounts this story of how the Prophet Muhammad scolded Fatima in the middle of the night after she requested a maidservant from war booty. Because Muslims were too poor to house and feed their prisoners of war, the prisoners became servants who could not leave at will. This form of slavery was common in the ancient world. The Prophet Muhammad had great compassion for those most vulnerable in society—slaves as well as widows and orphans—and received revelations from Allah concerning the just treatment of each.

S. C.

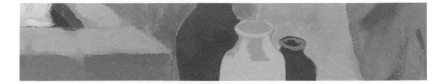

THE MERCHANT
BOYS' PRANK

In the Name of Allah, Most Gracious, Most Merciful:

O Prophet! Tell thy wives, your daughters, and the believing women that they should cast their outer garments over their persons (when out of doors): That is most convenient, that they should be known (as such) and not molested. And Allah is Oft-Forgiving, Most Merciful.
—Qur'an 33:59 (The Confederates)

Zarah stepped into the shade of the gold merchant's stall in Medina, the desert city where the Prophet Muhammad had migrated with his followers from Mecca. A woven goat-hair awning flapped in the summer sun. Peering through her sheer green veil, she pointed to the necklace with the amber stone.

"May I please see that one?" she asked the merchant, who wore fringed robes over plain garments beneath, in the style of a local Jewish tribe. A kaffiyeh covered most of his speckled gray hair. The goldsmith picked up the necklace and held it up to the sunlight. The stone flamed as if fire touched it.

"This is one of my finest," he said. "It arrived with yesterday's caravan. Would you like to try it on?"

"Yes," Zarah said, smiling as she took the necklace from him. Facing the back of the stall so the merchant could not see her, she unwrapped the veil that swaddled her face, shoulders, and upper body. Holding the ends of the chain on either side of her neck, she let the pendant dangle against her chest. Looking down at herself, she thought, *How lovely this looks against my skin.*

Two young men—about Zarah's age—from the neighboring stall joined the merchant beside a jewelry trunk. After watching Zarah fix her wraps, pulling her veil snugly about her face, one of them said, "Why bother to buy a necklace that no one will see, not even yourself?"

The older goldsmith glared at the youth. "Go back and mind your father's wares."

Zarah turned to the young man who questioned her. She noticed his unusual garb and the silly smirk on his face. She frowned at him and turned to the older merchant for help. Had he not had the reputation of the fairest jeweler in Medina, she would have left.

"He was just leaving," the goldsmith said, ushering the young man out by the elbow.

"Let him stay," Zarah said. "I will answer his question." She raised her chin. "I wear this veil for two reasons. First, it shelters me from the hot sun and blowing sand. Second, it shields me from the eyes of those who might mistake me for less than a respectable woman if I were not wearing it. An unveiled woman in Medina is sometimes thought by men to be one who offers herself to them."

The young man crossed his arms as Zarah continued. "People from many lands, with different customs, live here—Jews, Christians, Zoroastrians, and those who still worship idols. Others, like myself, follow the Prophet Muhammad, peace be upon him."

"So you wear that veil because Muhammad has told you to," the young man taunted. "Does he think nonbelievers like me are lowly, not worthy to look upon your face?" His dark eyes narrowed, his voice competing with the bazaar's clatter of hooves and the herders' whistles.

"The Prophet has not commanded me," Zarah said. "He only says that believing women should not display their adornments—and we should draw our veils over ourselves as this is more proper, so that we may be recognized as true believers and not be molested."

"Now you're saying that nonbelievers are all molesters?" The other young man leaned toward Zarah.

Zarah stepped closer to the older goldsmith, thinking, *Perhaps I should have let him send these two away.* But she continued. "You put words into the Prophet's mouth, and you suffer by them. I *choose* to wear my veil, as did my mother and grandmother who lived long before he was born."

Reluctantly, Zarah gave the necklace back to the gold merchant and said, "Thank you. I will come again when I have saved enough to buy it." Then she turned to the young men. "I do not ask you why you wear those robes, or that style of kaffiyeh, although I know it might have something to do with your faith. Perhaps you too worship the one God as Muslims do. We believe in that which has been revealed to Muhammad, and to Abraham, Moses, Jesus, and the other prophets by our God." Zarah raised her hands palms up and gestured to the north. "We pray facing Jerusalem." She glanced at the older Jewish merchant and smiled.

Looking directly into one young man's eyes, whose attention curiously seemed riveted on her, and with her back to the other, she continued. "Does not the Most Gracious, Most Merciful call upon you to offer me the same respect I have given you?"

Zarah thought she felt something rustle her garments. She lifted her hem from the earthen floor and looked from side to side, but nothing seemed amiss. She turned to leave and heard the sound of cloth ripping just as she felt a tug on her dress. The warmth of the sun and a breeze touched her exposed back. Looking over her shoulder, she saw the two young men laughing. A swatch of her torn robe hung from the jewelry trunk, where one of them had fastened it.

"Oh," gasped the goldsmith. "What have you done? Don't play your pranks on my customers! Get out of here!" he yelled at the two young men. "Get out of my stall!" Then he said to Zarah, as she gathered up the shreds of her robe, "I am sorry for your trouble. It will not happen again."

Although her blood pounded in her neck and her face burned, Zarah forced herself to keep quiet. *If I scream or run, I give them what they hoped for,* she thought, as she left the goldsmith's tent. Shaken, Zarah rearranged her veil to cover her bare back. Without a word, she walked to the fruit merchant across the square, as if to finish her shopping. *If I scream, I will bring misfortune to the undeserving goldsmith. I might even start a feud between my tribe and theirs.*

Hands trembling, she squeezed a pomegranate to test its ripeness, and thought about what she had heard last Friday in the olive grove where the Prophet Muhammad and her community gathered for prayer: "But great is the guilt of those who oppress their fellow men and conduct themselves with wickedness and injustice in the land."

Tears welled up in Zarah's eyes. *Why did those boys do this to me? I am veiled! I did not invite their attention.*

Then she remembered Muhammad's words. "If any show patience and forgive, that would truly be an affair of great resolution."

I will not cry, Zarah willed herself. *I will not,* she thought, as she paid the fruit merchant for her pomegranates and walked on.

ABOUT THE STORY

More than one version of the tale of an Arab woman who is the victim of a goldsmith's prank is included in modern and ancient texts surrounding the life of the Prophet Muhammad, peace be upon him. In this version the untold story is imagined: how the historically nameless victim, here called Zarah, speaks up for what she believes and chooses not to take offense and seek revenge. At the time of this story, the people of Medina had been living in peace, and Muslims prayed facing Jerusalem. (Years later, Muhammad would turn in the midst of prayer toward Mecca.) Later incidents like the one told here led to bloodshed between Muslims and other tribes in Medina.

The wearing of head coverings and veils was practiced long before the rise of Islam. They were worn by Christian and Jewish women as well as by women of many other faiths throughout the world for centuries. In some cases the scarves and veils showed the differences among social classes. Many women still wear them today.

M. N. S.

THE DOGS OF AL-HAW'AB

In the Name of Allah, Most Gracious, Most Merciful:

When the Qur'an is read, listen to it with attention, and hold your peace: that you may receive Mercy.
— *Qur'an 7:204 (The Heights)*

Aisha rose to greet her two visitors and nearly gasped. The faces of her sisters' husbands looked pained. A sense of foreboding stung at Aisha's chest, but her veil hid the expression on her face. *A wife of the Prophet Muhammad, peace be upon him,* she told herself, *must always demonstrate strength.*

That her brothers-in-law had come so far—all the way to the holy shrine at Mecca—could only mean serious trouble back home in Medina.

"Brothers, you have come a great distance. Come inside," Aisha coaxed, pretending to be calm. "Let me give you some cool water and dates for refreshment." She offered Zubair a welcoming hand, but instead, he grasped it and leaned closer.

"Sister," he said, "we have come with grim news. We must talk right away."

"Follow me," she said. Aisha led the men inside the small mud home in which she was staying. Removing their shoes as they entered, the three sat down on small leather mats. Aisha felt grateful being closer to solid ground—her knees felt like water.

"Sister," said Zubair, "as you know, several months ago the caliph, our leader, was murdered." He paused to emphasize his next point. "It is time to bring the murderers to justice. There is unrest at home and in the provinces. Everyone is divided."

Although her thoughts stormed, Aisha held silent. *Not since the Prophet died fourteen years ago have we faced a situation this serious—*

Talha's voice broke into her turbulent thoughts. "As the wife who lived closest to God's messenger," Talha said, "you have the authority to raise an army and find the murderers."

"You were always by the side of the Prophet, peace be upon him," insisted Zubair. "You know what he would have done in every situation."

Aisha passed each man a cupful of cool water. Zubair drank and then continued. "I believe men will listen to you. They will follow your command. With Allah's help you will lead us to justice."

Aisha had yet to determine a course of action. From childhood onward, she had been called Aisha the

Truthful for her ready opinions. But this time, only the barest tensing of her hands upon her knees disclosed her confusion. She felt like weeping at this impossible situation. *Our Muslim community is so young, and yet the seeds of division are watered with blood. Brother may end up fighting brother, and the murderers will have succeeded in splitting us apart!*

Waiting for her to think through her decision, both men sipped their water, their foreheads furrowed with concern. They gazed at the strip of blue sky seen through the narrow window. Aisha, too, looked out at the sky, searching her mind for words of guidance from the Prophet. *He always said that justice was second only to prayer.* The exact lines filled her ears, as if the Prophet were reciting right beside her: *"O you who believe! Stand out firmly for justice, as witnesses to Allah, even as against yourselves...or against your kin."*

Aisha felt a mixture of fear and purpose: She had known that her role as the Prophet's wife would be tested, but by leading an army? She forced herself to stand up. *"Inshallah*—by Allah's will—justice must prevail," she announced.

The midday sun shone fiercely. Hidden within her howdah, the tent over her saddle, Aisha felt as if she were baking inside an oven. Askar, her camel, was a beautiful thoroughbred—a gift to her for the campaign—yet even he labored in the heat. Plodding across the soft sand, his steps rocked her. She ached to close her eyes but fought against it. She was the leader of the hundreds of troops from Basra following behind her, and they had only just begun their march toward Medina.

To her left, a cluster of date palms signaled water. Waves of heat rose in vertical banners, making the trees appear to sway and dance. But it wasn't time for the troops to rest. Not yet. The scout had said another waterhole lay just two hours further.

As Aisha's camel passed the oasis, a dog bared his teeth and began to bark viciously. Then more and yet more joined, until it sounded as if a city of snarling dogs crouched just behind the palms. Aisha had never heard anything so strange before. The silky, fine hair of her forearms pricked and tingled.

She pulled aside the howdah's curtain to find Talha close by on horseback. "What spring is this, do you know?" she asked.

"It is al-Haw'ab, Sister."

Al-Haw'ab, al-Haw'ab. The name circled in her hazy state of mind, swinging back and forth with the camel's stride. *Al-Haw'ab!* Queasiness engulfed her; she clutched the rim of the howdah to keep from falling.

Now she remembered. A midsummer evening: the Prophet Muhammad among his wives, who were drawing lots to determine which woman would accompany him on his next journey. She had watched the Prophet's face alter. She could feel the sharp twist in her stomach again. Just before the Prophet had spoken, the room had fallen strangely silent—like birds before a sandstorm. It came back to her: He had warned her about the dogs at al-Haw'ab.

Aisha wrenched her camel to a stop. "Talha and Zubair!" she shouted. The two men pulled up beside her, reining in their horses. "We cannot go forward! The Prophet, peace be upon him, foresaw this situation—he saw that the dogs would be an omen of misfortune."

The two men listened to her hurried recounting of the story. The troops on foot would soon catch up. Aisha continued, "It can only mean that our campaign is doomed. We must halt the troops and retreat at once."

Despite the omen, the men pressed her onward. Barking dogs, they assured her, were not reason enough to turn back from such an important mission. She relented. After all, she was a woman with little military experience.

Now, only four days later, two opposing armies, hers against those of Ali, her son-in-law, stalled in an uneasy truce on a vast, sandy plain of Arabia. Their camps were separated by fewer than twenty camel strides. It was just as she had feared: kin against kin, although neither she nor Ali had played a role in the murder of the caliph.

Yesterday, Aisha had remained in her tent, praying to Allah, pleading for guidance. *Bless me with your instructions. What would the Prophet say? What would he do?*

For hours this afternoon, she and Ali, as well as their commanders, had met on a small rise overlooking the troops. Neither side wanted a bloody battle. Together they worked out a compromise to unify the Muslim community again.

Yet, strangely, when she had returned to her tent, her sense of dread from al-Haw'ab returned full force. There were too many soldiers, too many weapons—all of them too close. *And what if the Caliph's murderers try to defeat the compromise? What if they lead a sneak attack in the night to keep the community divided? What if, what if...*

Aisha could neither eat nor sleep. She knew that if a battle were to take place, it would be the first time two Muslim armies fought each other. *What if my own family dies at the hands of my men? My own brother, Muhammad, is in Ali's camp.* She wept when she thought this way. Sometimes it simply made her angry—how a small group of murderers had caused this turmoil among the followers of the Prophet.

It was after midnight. Ali's troops were so close that many of the night's sounds came from his army as well as hers. The bells of hobbled camels clanked at the camps' edges. Clothes rustled as men tossed in their sleep.

As she surveyed the plain under the stars, the blurred shapes of men and animals outlined the horizon in all directions. Some of the shapes moved, or seemed to make the darkness move. She blinked so that these tricks of the eyes would disappear.

The sun rose over the eastern horizon, infusing the battlefield with a bloody hue. Dozens of camels and horses lay dead on their sides across the wide field. Between them, the crumpled bodies of men lay motionless in the sand. Yet the battle was not over; men hid behind the small hillocks of their dead animals—desperate, holding out by firing every last arrow. Scores struggled man-to-man, some with swords, some without.

Even at this early hour, Aisha could see that the battle was not in their favor. The small patch dividing the two camps had long been overrun by Ali's army. When she had awakened, confused and disoriented in the predawn dark, to shouts, screams, and the clashing of swords, it was too late to determine how it started. Men were already dead and their companions seeking revenge. It was exactly the tragedy she had most feared.

The stench of blood grew strong in the warming sun. Like a horrible nightmare, the moans of wounded men and animals rose and fell. Wracked by uncertainty and fear, Aisha sensed that a terrible mistake had been made in the Prophet's name. *Not a single drop of blood*

165

from another mother's son should be shed for this. Somehow, the bloodshed must stop!

Aisha quickly joined her commanders, who were gathered toward the side of the plain. She could see that they, too, had misgivings. She broke the silence among them. "This battle should not have happened—we had finally come to a compromise."

The commanders looked at her, some faces blank, some puzzled. "What do you suggest, Sister?" asked the tall Qazi, the religious leader from Basra.

She looked up to the sky, as if pleading directly to Allah. She paused to gain her composure. "We must recall both sides, both armies to the will of Allah *now!*"

Aisha felt light-headed, almost dizzy. But some strength within called her to quick action. Unthinking, she ran to her camel, Askar, climbed up into the howdah, and gave the animal the sharp verbal command to rise. Aisha reined the camel straight into the battle. "*La ilaha illa 'llah*—There is no God but God," she uttered over and over, hoping that her prayer and presence would stop the fighting. Seventy of her men surrounded the camel, accompanying Aisha into the center of the storm.

She could hear the whine of arrows, followed by a ripping sound as they tore at the howdah's curtain. Through the rips in the curtain, Aisha saw that the men trying to protect her were failing against Ali's larger army. But she forced herself to steady her trembling hands and continue toward the battle's center.

Brought down by arrow and sword, Askar fell to his knees. The howdah toppled to the ground. Muhammad, Aisha's brother, ran to the howdah, reaching her before anyone else. When Aisha heard his concerned voice, a feeling of relief flooded her body. *It will end now!*

As Muhammad extended his hand to help her, all eyes, from both sides, watched. Aisha heard the fighting stop. When she straightened her robes and veil, looked at her brother and accepted his hand, all knew the battle was over.

"*Inshallah*, may Allah's will be done," she said.

ABOUT THE STORY

Aisha is undoubtedly one of the most fascinating and controversial women in Islamic history. Married to the Prophet Muhammad, peace be upon him, at a young age and outliving him, she participated in the tragic events leading to the first Muslim civil war. Although the reasons for the war were complicated, the problems were typical of those that arise during the building of any rapidly growing empire. Blame is not laid on either side. The battle portrayed in this story (held outside of Basra in the Muslim year 36, or 658 C.E.) is known as the Battle of the Camel, for Aisha was in the thick of the fighting, which did not stop until her camel, Askar, was killed.

Events have been condensed to tell this story, and conversations are fictionalized.

Because Aisha lived for fifty years after the Prophet's death, she became one of the most influential and respected authorities on questions of religion and the way a Muslim life should be led. She also had a considerable knowledge of ancient Arabic poetry, medicine, and genealogy. This knowledge, along with her many contributions to the Muslim Sunna (customs or fine examples of the Prophet), gave Muslim women an important role model in future years.

S. C.

FURTHER READING

Ali, Allma Abdullah Yusuf. *The Illustrious Qur'an,* sixth ed. Lahore: Sh. Muhammad Ashraf Publications, 2002.

Alter, Robert. *Genesis: Translation and Commentary.* New York: W. W. Norton & Company, 1996.

Armstrong, Carole. *Women of the Bible.* New York: Simon & Schuster, 1998.

Armstrong, Karen. *A History of God: The 4,000-Year Quest of Judaism, Christianity, and Islam.* New York: Ballantine, 1993.

————. *Islam: A Modern Library Chronicles Book.* New York: Modern Library, 2000.

Ashcroft, Mary Ellen. *Spirited Women: Encountering the First Women Believers.* Minneapolis: Augsburg Fortress Publications, 2000.

Bach, Alice, and J. Cheryl Exum. *Miriam's Well: Stories about Women in the Bible.* New York: Delacorte Press, 1991.

Bakhtiar, Laleh, and Shaykh Muhammad Hisham Kabbani. *Encyclopedia of Muhammad's Women Companions and the Traditions They Related.* Chicago: ABC International Group and Kazi Publications, 1998.

Biers-Ariel, Matt. *The Triumph of Eve: And Other Subversive Bible Tales.* Woodstock, Vt.: SkyLight Paths Publishing, 2004.

Birdseye, Debbie Holsclaw. *What I Believe: Kids Talk about Faith.* New York: Holiday House, 1996.

Bloch, Ariel, and Chana Bloch. *The Song of Songs: A New Translation.* New York: Random House, 1995.

Breuilly, Elizabeth. *Religions of the World: The Illustrated Guide to Origins, Beliefs, Traditions and Festivals.* New York: Facts on File, 1997.

Busse, Heribert. *Islam, Judaism, and Christianity: Theological and Historical Affiliations.* Princeton, N.J.: Markus Wiener Publishers, 1998.

Coogan, Michael D., ed. *The New Oxford Annotated Bible.* New York: Oxford University Press, 2001.

Cooper, John, trans. *The Commentary on the Qur'an,* vol. 1. London: Oxford University Press, 1987.

Deer, Edith. *All the Women of the Bible.* Edison, N.J.: Castle Books, 1955.

Dimont, Max I. *Jews, God, and History,* rev. and updated ed. New York: Penguin Books, 1994.

Al Faruqi, Lamya'. *Women, Muslim Society, and Islam.* Indianapolis: American Trust Publications, 1991.

Feiler, Bruce. *Abraham: A Journey to the Heart of Three Faiths.* New York: William Morrow, 2002.

Frankel, Ellen. *The Five Books of Miriam: A Woman's Commentary on the Torah.* New York: Grosset/Putnam, 1996.

Getty-Sullivan, Mary Ann. *Women in the New Testament.* Collegeville, Minn.: Liturgical Press, 2001.

Gibb, H.A.R., et al., eds. *The Encyclopedia of Islam,* vol. 1, new ed. London: Luzac and Company, 1960.

Ginzberg, Louis. *Legends of the Bible.* Philadelphia: Jewish Publication Society, 1992.

Goldstein, Elyse, ed. *The Women's Torah Commentary: New Insights from Women Rabbis on the Fifty-four Weekly Torah Portions.* Woodstock, Vt.: Jewish Lights Publishing, 2000.

Guillaume, A. *The Life of Muhammad: A Translation of Ishaq's Sirat Rasul Allah.* London: Oxford University Press, 1955.

Johnson, Elizabeth A. *She Who Is: The Mystery of God in Feminist Theological Discourse.* New York: Crossroad/ Herder & Herder, 1993.

Keane, Michael. *What You Will See Inside a Catholic Church.* Woodstock, Vt.: SkyLight Paths Publishing, 2002.

Khan, Aisha Karen. *What You Will See Inside a Mosque.* Woodstock, Vt.: SkyLight Paths Publishing, 2003.

Kvam, Kristen, Linda Schearing, and Valarie Ziegler, eds. *Eve and Adam: Jewish, Christian, and Muslim Readings on Genesis and Gender.* Indianapolis: Indiana University Press, 1999.

Mack, Stan. *The Story of the Jews: A 4,000-Year Adventure.* Woodstock, Vt.: Jewish Lights Publishing, 2001.

Matar, N. I. *Islam for Beginners.* New York: Writers and Readers, 1992.

McKenna, Megan. *Not Counting Women and Children: Neglected Stories from the Bible.* Maryknoll, N.Y.: Orbis Books.

Newsom, Carol A., and Sharon H. Ringe, eds. *The Women's Bible Commentary.* Louisville, Ky.: Westminster John Knox Press, 1998.

Osborne, Mary Pope. *One World, Many Religions: The Way We Worship.* New York: Knopf, 1996.

Phipps, William E. *Muhammad and Jesus.* New York: Continuum, 1999.

Rosen, Norma. *Biblical Women Unbound: Counter-tales.* Philadelphia: Jewish Publication Society, 1996.

Sardar, Ziauddin, and Zafar Abbas Malik. *Introducing Muhammad.* New York: Totem Books, 1997.

Sasso, Sandy Eisenberg. *But God Remembered: Stories of Women from Creation to the Promised Land*. Woodstock,Vt.: Jewish Lights Publishing, 1995.

Scholem, Gershom. *On the Kabbalah and Its Symbolism*. Translated by Ralph Manheim. New York: Schocken Books, 1996.

Spellberg, D. A. *Politics, Gender and the Islamic Past: The Legacy of A'isha bint Abi Baker*. New York: Columbia University Press, 1994.

Tanakh: A New Translation of the Holy Scriptures According to the Traditional Hebrew Text. Philadelphia: Jewish Publication Society, 1985.

Telushkin, Joseph. *Biblical Literacy: The Most Important People, Events, and Ideas of the Hebrew Bible*. New York: William Morrow and Company, 1997.

Walther, Wiebke. *Women in Islam: From Medieval to Modern Times*. Princeton, N.J.: Markus Wiener Publishers, 1999.

Ward, Kaari, ed. *Jesus and His Times*. Pleasantville, N.Y.: Readers' Digest, 1987.

Watt, W. Montgomery, and M.V. McDonald. *The History of al-Tabari*. New York: Sate University of New York Press, 1988.

What You Will See Inside a Synagogue. Woodstock, Vt.: SkyLight Paths Publishing, 2004.

Wilkinson, Philip. *Islam (Eyewitness Guide)*. London and New York: Dorling Kindersley, 2002.

Yakun, Fathi. *To Be a Muslim*. Indianapolis: American Trust Publications.

AUTHORS' NOTE

This book evolved from the place where our own spiritual journeys intersected. The women of these stories aroused our curiosity and drew us together. Some
were well known, others unnamed. All were women
who spoke to us because, like ourselves, they too had
struggled with doubt and wrestled with their faith. Some
we chose for the roles that we shared with them, such as
Shiphrah, a midwife; Lydia, a weaver; and Salome, a
mother. As mothers, we wanted to find spiritual role
models for our daughters as much as for ourselves.

We began with the women of the Jewish and
Christian traditions in which we were raised. Then we
came upon Hagar. Like Sarah, she also conceived a son
of Abraham. Her son, Ishmael, is the ancestor of the
Prophet Muhammad, the founder of Islam. Hagar
coaxed us out of our familiar places and compelled us
to embrace another branch of the family tree. She
introduced us to Khadija, Fatima, Aisha, and Zarah.

As a community of writers we encouraged and
nudged, challenged and supported one another. In

drafting the stories, we consulted scholars from all three religious traditions, whose input and interpretations pushed us beyond our biases and assumptions.

SARAH L. CONOVER has long-standing interests in world religions and education. Her book *Kindness: Buddhist Wisdom for Children and Parents* was chosen as one of the best spiritual books for children of 2002 by ALA's *Booklist*. *Ayat Jamilah: Beautiful Signs, a Treasury of Islamic Wisdom for Children and Parents* won the 2004 Aesop Prize. She is also the author of *At Work in Life's Garden: Essays on Growing the Soul through Parenting*. She holds a B.A. in religious studies from the University of Colorado and an M.F.A. in creative writing from Eastern Washington University. Sarah has traveled worldwide, producing award-winning documentaries for PBS, the Discovery Channel, and the United Nations. Currently she teaches high school language arts in Spokane, Washington.

MARY CRONK FARRELL (www.MaryCronkFarrell.com), a former award-winning TV journalist, now writes a syndicated column on family spirituality, and is author of *Celebrating Faith: Year-Round Activities for Catholic Families; Fire in the Hole!*, a historical novel for young readers; and numerous newspaper and magazine articles. She is a frequent speaker at women's retreats and religious conferences, and she is one of a team of regular preachers in her parish. She is married and the mother of three children.

CLAIRE RUDOLF MURPHY (www.ClaireRudolfMurphy.com) is the author of several books for children and young adults. Her *Children of the Gold Rush* won the 2000 Willa Cather Award for best juvenile nonfiction book of the West. Among her other award-winning books are *I Am Sacajawea, I Am York: Our Journey West with Lewis and Clark; Caribou Girl; Gold Rush Women;* and *A Child's Alaska.* Her novel, *Free Radical,* was published by Clarion Books in 2002. Claire lived twenty-four years in Alaska, where she learned about the many native Alaskan cultures that are featured in her books. She taught for three years in the Yup'ik Eskimo village of St. Mary's, where she and her husband served as Jesuit volunteers. Claire and her family returned to her hometown of Spokane, Washington, in 1998, where she writes, works with teachers and students, and studies Scripture.

MEGHAN NUTTALL SAYRES (www.MeghanNuttallSayres.com) is a tapestry weaver whose Celtic Christian heritage and interest in desert cultures have led her to hermitages and holy wells of Ireland and carpet-weaving villages in Turkey and Iran. Her poetry and essays have appeared in journals such as *Orion* and *New Hibernia Review.* She is author of a children's book, *The Shape of Bettes Meadow: A Wetlands Story.* Her first novel, *Anahita's Woven Riddle* is forthcoming. She lives in Valleyford, Washington, with her family, two cats, two sheep, and a prayer rug.

BETSY WHARTON is a candidate for the M.F.A. degree in creative writing at Eastern Washington University. Her essay "The Rabbi's Garage" was a winner of the AWP Intro Award in 2001. Betsy was raised in a Presbyterian family and then married into the Jewish tradition. She has worked as a registered nurse in Islamic Pakistan, in a Seattle hospice for persons with AIDS, and on the Navajo Indian Reservation. Currently she is working with high-risk mothers and infants in Port Angeles, Washington, where she resides with her husband and two children.

ACKNOWLEDGMENTS

I am, and always will be, grateful to my husband, Doug Robnett, for his steady support, humor, and wisdom. I would also like to thank my mother, Fran Church, for her exemplary happiness. Several people have generously helped me, a respectful outsider to their religions, in researching and developing stories appropriate to their traditions: Dr. Freda Crane of the Islamic Society of North America, Fatima Ansari of the Spokane Islamic Society, and Sam Schnall of Spokane, Washington.

S. C.

I would like to thank my parents, Harold and Margaret Cronk, for starting me on the path of faith; and the Scripture study and faith-sharing groups I've journeyed with during the past twenty years for loving me into a deeper experience of that faith. I would like to acknowledge Joy Milos, C.S.J., whose spirituality classes at Gonzaga University stretched my mind and fed my soul; and Linda Kobe-Smith, my pastor, for her model of courage and faith. I would also like to thank the

Catholic Community of St. Ann for being like family, challenging me to grow, and recognizing and nurturing my gifts.

M. C. F.

Since these stories have been composting in my mind since childhood, I would like to thank my parents, the nuns at St. Augustine's and Holy Names Academy, my professors at Santa Clara University, and my experiences in the Jesuit Volunteer Corps at St. Mary's Mission in Alaska. Discussion and study with my prayer group in Fairbanks, the Sacred Heart scripture class, and my childhood friends in the Wisdom Circle have also helped me search out these stories. My husband, children, and extended family members have blessed me on my writing journey. Thanks to Father Elias Chacour, who inspired us with his eloquent words about the common roots of all three religions, and to Sam Schnall. Maura D. Shaw and Jon Sweeney at SkyLight Paths helped our vision become reality.

C. R. M.

I would like to thank my friends Mojdeh Khalighi and Farhad Kashcfi for their suggestions on some of the Muslim women's stories in this collection, as well as the scholars mentioned above by my coauthor Sarah Conover. Thanks also to Reuven Prager, Levite on

Duty, Beged Ivri, Jerusalem, for his thoughts on inter-faith dialogue and assistance with questions on ancient clothing. Thanks to our editor, Maura D. Shaw; to the staff at the North Spokane County Library for their consistent enthusiasm; and to my family and friends for all of their support.

M. N. S.

My thanks go out to my mother, Betty Wharton, who kindled the flame that still burns inside me.

B. W.

READER'S
DISCUSSION GUIDE

GENERAL TOPICS

Each of the women in these stories has a strong voice for her faith. Is it more difficult for some women than for others to speak out? Why?

The stories come from the three monotheistic religions that descended from the patriarch Abraham. What do you learn about the relationships among the three religions, in their history, practices or beliefs? Do you see any connections that you have not seen before?

Close friendships play an important role in the lives of most women, whether in ancient times or today. Of all the women in these stories, who do you think might become close friends if that were possible? Why?

JEWISH STORIES

A Thousand Wrinkles (Sarah)

In this story, do you think Sarah acts from jealousy, as is often depicted? What other motivations does she have for asking Abraham to cast out Ishmael and Hagar?

If Sarah is intended by God to play a certain role at this time, how hard is it for her to accept that role? What troubles her?

How would you feel if you had to choose between two sons: one to receive great benefit and the other to confront unknown challenges? Are there instances in modern life where women have to make similar decisions about their children?

River Journey (Shiphrah)

When this story begins, Shiphrah is an Egyptian who has little sympathy for the Hebrew slaves. How does she change over the course of the story? What inspires that change?

What Pharaoh tells the midwives to do would be considered infanticide—murder—in our culture. How do the Egyptian women react to his order? How do you think you might react in the same circumstances?

The chant of the Hebrew woman in labor seems to have special meaning both for her and for the midwife. Are there prayers, chants or songs that you have used to help you through difficult situations?

A Dance in the Desert (Miriam)

Even though she is the sister of Moses, Miriam sometimes gets weary of her role as elder sister. Is Miriam becoming a bitter old woman? Why might that happen?

Do you think that Miriam is justified in her anger at God? Are you ever angry at God? What do you do about it?

What returns the joy to Miriam's life? What does she have to let go of before she can dance again?

The Pool of Siloam (Huldah)

Would you consider Huldah to be the most important woman in the history of the Jewish religion? Why or why not?

Huldah's visions are terrifying and might stop anyone else from continuing the task of validating the scroll. What gives her the courage to continue?

Huldah takes comfort in knowing that the children of Israel will continue their Covenant with God no matter what happens to the Temple. How has this vision proved true?

O Come My Beloved (Shoshana)

This story is more of a fable than most other stories in the book. What do you learn from the journey of each of the lovers searching for one another? What does their love symbolize?

The evening ritual that Shoshana's grandmother taught her had been done since "the first days of Creation." Is it a ritual familiar to you? How are women today passing down their rituals to their daughters and sons?

▪ The ending of the story is not a happy one. Were you surprised? What hope and possibility does it offer?

Return to Hadassah (Esther)

▪ The young woman who changes her name to Esther relies on her beauty for success in life. How does Esther truly grow into her strength? How does she become more than a queen?

▪ When Esther is preparing herself to make her request to the king, she fasts and asks the Jewish people of the city to do so, too. Have you ever incorporated the ritual of fasting into your life? What was your experience?

▪ Esther knows that she could be killed for approaching the king without an invitation, yet she trusts in God's will for her and puts aside her fear. What are some other examples of women—in history or in modern life— who have placed their trust in God and been able to do courageous or remarkable things?

CHRISTIAN STORIES

Woman to Woman (Mary of Nazareth)

▪ In this story, Mary is ambivalent about the miraculous blessing God bestowes upon her. Yet through her willingness to accept her role in God's plan, she proves her worthiness. Have you ever been in a situation in which you accepted a responsibility that you did not feel prepared to handle? What happened?

Mary empathizes with Hannah, the mother of the prophet Samuel, in the heartbreak of giving a son exclusively over to God's work. Mary and her cousin Elizabeth both experience this anguish firsthand. What spiritual gifts are required to be a mother who can sacrifice so much? Are mothers today still confronted with this challenge? How?

Mary promises herself to look for joy in each new day, despite her uncertain future. Do you think she continued this practice through her life? How does the search for joy influence the spiritual lives of people?

Crumbs from the Table (Eleni)

Eleni is single-minded in her determination to find Jesus the healer in order to ask him to restore her daughter to health, which he does because of Eleni's faith. In our daily lives, not everything we ask of God is granted, no matter how hard we pray. What is the meaning of faith for us in this context?

In this story, Jesus is portrayed with human traits such as impatience, and he realizes a significant component of his spiritual mission through his encounter with the Gentile woman. Does it surprise you to see Jesus depicted with fallible characteristics, being liable to make a mistake or a hasty judgment? Why or why not? What did he learn from his encounter with the Gentile woman?

▣ Eleni's behavior might be seen as rude and overbearing, even manipulative. Does her desperation justify her behavior? Have you ever met someone who seemed to act rudely but actually helped you to learn an important life lesson?

Will I Drink of His Cup? (Salome)

▣ Salome is shocked by Jesus's teaching of forgiveness for one's enemies. What does she find so peculiar—the idea of forgiveness or the lack of retaliation and revenge? What consequences would forgiving one's enemies have?

▣ Like many mothers, Salome is proud of her sons and is fiercely protective at the same time. Why do you think her sons try to "manage" their mother when she approaches Jesus? Are they more concerned about what she will say to Jesus or about what Jesus might say to her? Have you ever been in a similar situation with your own child or parent?

▣ Salome's eyes are at last opened to see treasures beyond earthly riches. How do we prevent material concerns from interfering with our spiritual growth? What actions can we take to serve the poor, the hungry, the vulnerable?

Servant to Truth (Binah)

▣ The servants at the house of Caiaphas work long hours and are roughly treated. Binah feels that she and other poor people are not being protected by God as was promised. What might be her response to Jesus's message to the poor and the powerless?

Binah engages in a behavior that is common to many people who feel abused and victimized—she blames others for her own mistakes. Yet when the light of love and understanding is ignited in her heart, we know that she will change that behavior. How can we help ourselves and others to maintain this love and understanding?

The servant girl whose question prompts Peter to deny knowing Jesus plays a role in bringing about the fulfillment of the prophecy. In this story, Binah receives a healing of her spirit through her brief contacts with Jesus. Is this healing a result of her growing compassion and empathy, or is it in return for her part in fulfilling the prophecy? Has a brief encounter with someone ever made a profound difference in your life?

Love Casts Out Fear (Mary Magdalene)

What do you think is the significance of Mary Magdalene being the first person to see Jesus after he rose from the tomb? Does it have a broader meaning for the role of women in Christian churches?

How does Mary Magdalene have the courage to leave the upstairs room where the disciples are in hiding? Why do you think she is willing to risk her life to complete the anointing of Jesus's body?

185

Jesus tells Mary Magdalene that faith, not understanding, is required to accept his triumph over death. What are the key differences between faith and understanding? Which of the two is harder for you to practice?

Weaving a Church (Lydia)

One of the clear messages of Lydia's story is about the work of the hands supporting the work of the spirit. If you do a craft such as knitting, crocheting or weaving, have you ever practiced it with spiritual intent? Have you ever created handmade articles to be sold or raffled to raise funds to help others? Do you feel differently about those articles as you create them? Through what other activities can the spirit be supported by the hands? How?

As Paul points out in his letter, love is most important. Where there is love, there is no place for competition. Have you known people who compete over their level of religiousness? Have you known people whose generosity and openness are inspirational? What strengths does it take in you to bear with the former and learn from the latter?

Does it seem easy for Lydia to transfer her skills as a dye-master, weaver and merchant to help organize a growing church? Are there individuals in your community who serve their religious organizations by using their business or technical skills? Their artistic skills? Where and how could you be most valuable?

MUSLIM STORIES

The Night Wind (Eve)

In this story both Eve and Adam eat from the forbidden fruit at the same time after they are deceived by the beautiful Iblis. In your opinion, how does this change the interpretation of the story?

Eve's long walk of punishment and exile from Adam is made bearable by the sense that Allah's presence is still with her. Her repentance is sincere, so she is permitted to enter Mecca and reunite with her beloved. Why is exile and abandonment such a serious punishment for humans? How do we keep in touch with God as we work through our repentance?

The sanctification and purification rituals prescribed for Adam and Eve are still practiced in the religion of Islam today. Do you participate in any similar rituals in your faith tradition? How meaningful are the rituals in your life?

The Waters of Zamzam (Hagar)

In this version, the exile of Ishmael and Hagar occurs when Ishmael is a baby. Does that make the exile seem crueler? Does it give a greater role to Ishmael, whose baby feet opened the well at Zamzam, as the founder of the Arab people? How does it change the focus on Hagar, from a spiritual perspective?

Hagar submits to the will of Abraham when he assures her that it is also the will of Allah. Her complete trust in God provides rescue for her and her son from certain death. How hard do you find it to step back and wait for God's will to become clear? Do you run from hill to hill like Hagar before calling out to God?

Hagar creates a beautiful oasis of welcome around the holy spring at Zamzam. How can you create a sacred space where God is always present and where people can find spiritual nourishment? Can you embody that space yourself, becoming the welcomer? Can you join with others in meditation, prayer or music to create a sacred space for all present?

A Faith Blossoms (Khadija)

Alone on Mount Hira, Khadija experiences a direct personal relationship with God. She stops her busy life long enough to listen. Do we need to make special efforts to find times of silence in which we can be more open to listening to God? Maybe we can't climb to a mountaintop, or spend days alone in a retreat, but what *can* we do?

Khadija risks the ridicule of others and possible damage to her business by asking to pray as a follower of the Prophet Muhammad. What, if anything, do we risk today if we speak publicly about our spiritual lives?

Khadija rejoices in her ability to financially support her husband, Muhammad, so that he can fulfill his role as

Prophet. It is said that she is the one who proposed to him and that she manipulated her father into agreeing to the marriage. Do you see many different ways in which God provides, as the Prophet says? Has someone ever smoothed the way for you to accomplish something you believed in? Have you had the opportunity to do that for others? How can we act as God's hands?

Prayers in the Darkness (Fatima)

Fatima and her family live simple lives, perhaps even in poverty at times. This must have been different from her childhood as Khadija's youngest daughter. What do you think about her request for a servant to help her? How far should voluntary poverty or self-sacrifice extend?

Fatima's children are well-schooled in their grandfather's religious faith and accept their special responsibilities as the family of the Prophet. Do you think that passing down religious faith and tradition is one of the more important roles of women? How have the challenges of doing so changed in modern times?

Fatima finds peace in praising Allah as her father instructed. Have you ever used repetitive prayer or chant as a way of deepening spiritually or of finding comfort? What was the experience like?

The Merchant Boys' Prank (Zarah)

Do you think that Zarah shows maturity and bravery in explaining to the two young men why she wears a veil?

Or is she naïve in thinking she will be heard by people who want to tease and humiliate her? Have you ever experienced a similar situation of being taunted or tricked? How did you handle it? What did you learn from it?

Zarah makes a conscious decision to control her feelings and to keep her dignity, rather than cry out in protest at her treatment. She follows the Prophet's injunction to forgive and to remain patient. It is a struggle for her. Do you struggle with suppressing justified anger? Are there times when forgiveness and patience are the better responses? Are there times when protest is the better response?

Women have worn veils and head coverings throughout history, sometimes by choice, sometimes not. If you wear or have worn a veil or headscarf in a religious context, did it make you feel different about yourself? Did it set you apart in some way other than merely by outward appearence? How did others react?

The Dogs of al-Haw'ab (Aisha)

This first battle between Muslim factions foretold a division in Islam that continues to this day, between the Shi'a and Sunni sects. What do you think the Prophet Muhammad meant by saying that justice was second only to prayer? In your opinion, what options does the world have in achieving justice?

Aisha is not able to avert the battle, although she has the warning of disaster, because she is a woman without military experience and does not trust her own judgment. Could she have done anything differently? What might you have done in her place?

Her courage and faith made Aisha a role model for Muslim women through the centuries. Who have been your role models, whether in your own faith tradition or in another? How did their spiritual strengths influence their actions—and yours?

AVAILABLE FROM BETTER BOOKSTORES.
TRY YOUR BOOKSTORE FIRST.

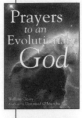

Meditation / Prayer

Prayers to an Evolutionary God
by William Cleary; Afterword by Diarmuid O'Murchu
How is it possible to pray when God is dislocated from heaven, dispersed all around us, and more of a creative force than an all-knowing father? Inspired by the spiritual and scientific teachings of Diarmuid O'Murchu and Teilhard de Chardin, Cleary reveals that religion and science can be combined to create an expanding view of the universe—an evolutionary faith.
6 x 9, 208 pp, HC, ISBN 1-59473-006-7 **$21.99**

The Song of Songs: A Spiritual Commentary
by M. Basil Pennington, OCSO; Illustrations by Phillip Ratner
Join M. Basil Pennington as he ruminates on the Bible's most challenging mystical text. You will follow a path into the Songs that weaves through his inspired words and the evocative drawings of Jewish artist Phillip Ratner—a path that reveals your own humanity and leads to the deepest delight of your soul.
6 x 9, 160 pp, HC, 14 b/w illus., ISBN 1-59473-004-0 **$19.99**

Women of Color Pray: Voices of Strength, Faith, Healing, Hope, and Courage   *Edited and with Introductions by Christal M. Jackson*
Through these prayers, poetry, lyrics, meditations and affirmations, you will share in the strong and undeniable connection women of color share with God. It will challenge you to explore new ways of prayerful expression.
5 x 7¼, 240 pp, Quality PB, ISBN 1-59473-077-6 **$15.99**

The Art of Public Prayer, 2nd Edition: Not for Clergy Only
by Lawrence A. Hoffman   6 x 9, 288 pp, Quality PB, ISBN 1-893361-06-3 **$18.95**

Finding Grace at the Center: The Beginning of Centering Prayer
by M. Basil Pennington, ocso, Thomas Keating, ocso, and Thomas E. Clarke, SJ
5 x 7¼, 112 pp, HC, ISBN 1-893361-69-1 **$14.95**

A Heart of Stillness: A Complete Guide to Learning the Art of Meditation
by David A. Cooper   5½ x 8½, 272 pp, Quality PB, ISBN 1-893361-03-9 **$16.95**

Meditation without Gurus: A Guide to the Heart of Practice
by Clark Strand   5½ x 8½, 192 pp, Quality PB, ISBN 1-893361-93-4 **$16.95**

Praying with Our Hands: Twenty-One Practices of Embodied Prayer from the
World's Spiritual Traditions   *by Jon M. Sweeney; Photographs by Jennifer J. Wilson; Foreword by Mother Tessa Bielecki; Afterword by Taitetsu Unno, PhD*
8 x 8, 96 pp, 22 duotone photographs, Quality PB, ISBN 1-893361-16-0 **$16.95**

Silence, Simplicity & Solitude: A Complete Guide to Spiritual Retreat at Home
by David A. Cooper   5½ x 8½, 336 pp, Quality PB, ISBN 1-893361-04-7 **$16.95**

Three Gates to Meditation Practice: A Personal Journey into Sufism, Buddhism,
and Judaism   *by David A. Cooper*   5½ x 8½, 240 pp, Quality PB, ISBN 1-893361-22-5 **$16.95**

Women Pray: Voices through the Ages, from Many Faiths, Cultures, and Traditions
Edited and with introductions by Monica Furlong
5 x 7¼, 256 pp, Quality PB, ISBN 1-59473-071-7 **$15.99**;
Deluxe HC with ribbon marker, ISBN 1-893361-25-X **$19.95**

Or phone, fax, mail or e-mail to: SKYLIGHT PATHS Publishing
Sunset Farm Offices, Route 4 • P.O. Box 237 • Woodstock, Vermont 05091
Tel: (802) 457-4000 • Fax: (802) 457-4004 • www.skylightpaths.com
Credit card orders: (800) 962-4544 (8:30AM–5:30PM ET Monday–Friday)
Generous discounts on quantity orders. SATISFACTION GUARANTEED. Prices subject to change.

Children's Spiritual Biography

MULTICULTURAL, NONDENOMINATIONAL, NONSECTARIAN

Ten Amazing People
And How They Changed the World
by Maura D. Shaw; Foreword by Dr. Robert Coles
Full-color illus. by Stephen Marchesi

For ages 7 & up

Black Elk • Dorothy Day • Malcolm X • Mahatma Gandhi • Martin Luther King, Jr. • Mother Teresa • Janusz Korczak • Desmond Tutu • Thich Nhat Hanh • Albert Schweitzer

This vivid, inspirational, and authoritative book will open new possibilities for children by telling the stories of how ten of the past century's greatest leaders changed the world in important ways.

8½ x 11, 48 pp, HC, Full-color illus., ISBN 1-893361-47-0 **$17.95** *For ages 7 & up*

Spiritual Biographies for Young People—For ages 7 and up

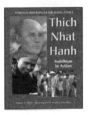
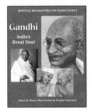
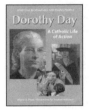
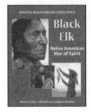

Black Elk: Native American Man of Spirit
by Maura D. Shaw; Full-color illus. by Stephen Marchesi
Through historically accurate illustrations and photos, inspiring age-appropriate activities, and Black Elk's own words, this colorful biography introduces children to a remarkable person who ensured that the traditions and beliefs of his people would not be forgotten.
6¾ x 8¾, 32 pp, HC, Full-color illus., ISBN 1-59473-043-1 **$12.99**

Dorothy Day: A Catholic Life of Action
by Maura D. Shaw; Full-color illus. by Stephen Marchesi
Introduces children to one of the most inspiring women of the twentieth century, a down-to-earth spiritual leader who saw the presence of God in every person she met. Includes practical activities, a timeline, and a list of important words to know.
6¾ x 8¾, 32 pp, HC, Full-color illus., ISBN 1-59473-011-3 **$12.99**

Gandhi: India's Great Soul
by Maura D. Shaw; Full-color illus. by Stephen Marchesi
There are a number of biographies of Gandhi written for young readers, but this is the only one that balances a simple text with illustrations, photographs, and activities that encourage children and adults to talk about how to make changes happen without violence. Introduces children to important concepts of freedom, equality, and justice among people of all backgrounds and religions.
6¾ x 8¾, 32 pp, HC, Full-color illus., ISBN 1-893361-91-8 **$12.95**

Thich Nhat Hanh: Buddhism in Action
by Maura D. Shaw; Full-color illus. by Stephen Marchesi
Warm illustrations, photos, age-appropriate activities, and Thich Nhat Hanh's own poems introduce a great man to children in a way they can understand and enjoy. Includes a list of important Buddhist words to know.
6¾ x 8¾, 32 pp, HC, Full-color illus., ISBN 1-893361-87-X **$12.95**

Children's Spirituality

ENDORSED BY CATHOLIC, PROTESTANT, JEWISH, AND BUDDHIST RELIGIOUS LEADERS

God Said Amen
by Sandy Eisenberg Sasso; Full-color illus. by Avi Katz
A warm and inspiring tale of two kingdoms that shows us that we need only reach out to each other to find the answers to our prayers.
9 x 12, 32 pp, HC, Full-color illus., ISBN 1-58023-080-6 **$16.95**
For ages 4 & up (a Jewish Lights book)

How Does God Listen?
by Kay Lindahl; Full-color photo illus. by Cynthia Maloney
How do we know when God is listening to us? Children will find the answers to these questions as they engage their senses while the story unfolds, learning how God listens in the wind, waves, clouds, hot chocolate, perfume, our tears and our laughter.
10 x 8½, 32 pp, Quality PB, Full-color photo illus., ISBN 1-59473-084-9 **$8.99**
For ages 3–6

In God's Name
by Sandy Eisenberg Sasso; Full-color illus. by Phoebe Stone
Like an ancient myth in its poetic text and vibrant illustrations, this award-winning modern fable about the search for God's name celebrates the diversity and, at the same time, the unity of all the people of the world.
9 x 12, 32 pp, HC, Full-color illus., ISBN 1-879045-26-5 **$16.95**
For ages 4 & up (a Jewish Lights book)

Also available in Spanish:
El nombre de Dios
9 x 12, 32 pp, HC, Full-color illus., ISBN 1-893361-63-2 **$16.95**

Where Does God Live?
by August Gold; Full-color photo illus. by Matthew J. Perlman
Using simple, everyday examples that children can relate to, this colorful book helps young readers develop a personal understanding of God.
10 x 8½, 32 pp, Quality PB, Full-color photo illus., ISBN 1-893361-39-X **$8.99**
For ages 3–6

In Our Image: God's First Creatures
by Nancy Sohn Swartz; Full-color illus. by Melanie Hall
A playful new twist on the Creation story—from the perspective of the animals. Celebrates the interconnectedness of nature and the harmony of all living things.   9 x 12, 32 pp, HC, Full-color illus., ISBN 1-879045-99-0 **$16.95**
For ages 4 & up (a Jewish Lights book)

Noah's Wife: The Story of Naamah
by Sandy Eisenberg Sasso; Full-color illus. by Bethanne Andersen
This new story, based on an ancient text, opens readers' religious imaginations to new ideas about the well-known story of the Flood. When God tells Noah to bring the animals of the world onto the ark, God also calls on Naamah, Noah's wife, to save each plant on Earth.
9 x 12, 32 pp, HC, Full-color illus., ISBN 1-58023-134-9 **$16.95**
For ages 4 & up (a Jewish Lights book)

Also available:
Naamah: Noah's Wife (A Board Book)
by Sandy Eisenberg Sasso, Full-color illus by Bethanne Andersen
5 x 5, 24 pp, Board Book, Full-color illus., ISBN 1-893361-56-X **$7.99** *For ages 0–4*

Children's Spirituality

ENDORSED BY CATHOLIC, PROTESTANT, JEWISH, AND BUDDHIST RELIGIOUS LEADERS

Because Nothing Looks Like God

by Lawrence and Karen Kushner; Full-color illus. by Dawn W. Majewski
Real-life examples of happiness and sadness—from goodnight stories, to
the hope and fear felt the first time at bat, to the closing moments of life—
introduce children to the possibilities of spiritual life.

11 x 8½, 32 pp, HC, Full-color illus., ISBN 1-58023-092-X **$16.95**

For ages 4 & up (a Jewish Lights book)

Also available:

Teacher's Guide, 8½ x 11, 22 pp, PB, ISBN 1-58023-140-3 **$6.95** For ages 5–8

Becoming Me: A Story of Creation

by Martin Boroson; Full-color illus. by Christopher Gilvan-Cartwright
Told in the personal "voice" of the Creator, here is a story about creation and
relationship that is about each one of us.
8 x 10, 32 pp, Full-color illus., HC, ISBN 1-893361-11-X **$16.95** For ages 4 & up

But God Remembered: Stories of Women from Creation to the

Promised Land   by Sandy Eisenberg Sasso; Full-color illus. by Bethanne Andersen
A fascinating collection of four different stories of women only briefly mentioned
in biblical tradition and religious texts; all teach important values through their
actions and faith.   9 x 12, 32 pp, HC, Full-color illus., ISBN 1-879045-43-5 **$16.95**
For ages 8 & up (a Jewish Lights book)

Cain & Abel: Finding the Fruits of Peace

by Sandy Eisenberg Sasso; Full-color illus. by Joani Keller Rothenberg
A sensitive recasting of the ancient tale shows we have the power to deal with anger
in positive ways. Provides questions for kids and adults to explore together.
"Editor's Choice"—American Library Association's *Booklist*

9 x 12, 32 pp, HC, Full-color illus., ISBN 1-58023-123-3 **$16.95** For ages 5 & up (a Jewish Lights book)

Does God Hear My Prayer?

by August Gold; Full-color photo illus. by Diane Hardy Waller
This colorful book introduces preschoolers as well as young readers to prayer
and how prayer can help them express their own fears, wants, sadness, surprise,
and joy.   10 x 8½, 32 pp, Quality PB, Full-color photo illus., ISBN 1-59473-102-0 **$8.99**

The 11th Commandment: Wisdom from Our Children

by The Children of America
"If there were an Eleventh Commandment, what would it be?" Children of
many religious denominations across America answer this question—in their
own drawings and words. "A rare book of spiritual celebration for all people, of
all ages, for all time." —*Bookviews*

8 x 10, 48 pp, HC, Full-color illus., ISBN 1-879045-46-X **$16.95** For ages 4 & up (a Jewish Lights book)

For Heaven's Sake

by Sandy Eisenberg Sasso; Full-color illus. by Kathryn Kunz Finney
Everyone talked about heaven: "Thank heavens." "Heaven forbid." "For heav-
en's sake, Isaiah." But no one would say what heaven was or how to find it. So
Isaiah decides to find out, by seeking answers from many different people.

9 x 12, 32 pp, HC, Full-color illus., ISBN 1-58023-054-7 **$16.95** For ages 4 & up (a Jewish Lights book)

God in Between

by Sandy Eisenberg Sasso; Full-color illus. by Sally Sweetland
If you wanted to find God, where would you look? A magical, mythical tale that
teaches that God can be found where we are: within all of us and the relationships
between us.   9 x 12, 32 pp, HC, Full-color illus., ISBN 1-879045-86-9 **$16.95**
For ages 4 & up (a Jewish Lights book)

Spirituality

Autumn: A Spiritual Biography of the Season
Edited by Gary Schmidt and Susan M. Felch; Illustrations by Mary Azarian
Autumn is a season of fruition and harvest, of thanksgiving and celebration of abundance and goodness of the earth. But it is also a season that starkly and realistically encourages us to see the limitations of our time. Warm and poignant pieces by Wendell Berry, David James Duncan, Robert Frost, A. Bartlett Giamatti, Kimiko Hahn, P. D. James, Julian of Norwich, Garret Keizer, Tracy Kidder, Anne Lamott, May Sarton, and many others rejoice in autumn as a time of preparation and reflection. 6 x 9, 320 pp, 5 b/w illus., HC, ISBN 1-59473-005-9 **$22.99**

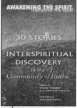

Awakening the Spirit, Inspiring the Soul
30 Stories of Interspiritual Discovery in the Community of Faiths
Edited by Brother Wayne Teasdale and Martha Howard, MD; Foreword by Joan Borysenko, PhD
Thirty original spiritual mini-biographies that showcase the varied ways that people come to faith—and what that means—in today's multi-religious world.
6 x 9, 224 pp, HC, ISBN 1-59473-039-3 **$21.99**

Winter: A Spiritual Biography of the Season
Edited by Gary Schmidt and Susan M. Felch; Illustrations by Barry Moser
Delves into the varied feelings that winter conjures in us, calling up both the barrenness and the beauty of the natural world in wintertime. Includes selections by

Will Campbell, Rachel Carson, Annie Dillard, Donald Hall, Ron Hansen, Jane Kenyon, Jamaica Kincaid, Barry Lopez, Kathleen Norris, John Updike, E. B. White, and many others. "This outstanding anthology features top-flight nature and spirituality writers on the fierce, inexorable season of winter.... Remarkably lively and warm, despite the icy subject." —*Publishers Weekly* Starred Review
6 x 9, 288 pp, 6 b/w illus., Deluxe PB w/flaps, ISBN 1-893361-92-6 **$18.95**; HC, ISBN 1-893361-53-5 **$21.95**

The Alphabet of Paradise: An A–Z of Spirituality for Everyday Life
by Howard Cooper 5 x 7¼, 224 pp, Quality PB, ISBN 1-893361-80-2 **$16.95**

Creating a Spiritual Retirement: A Guide to the Unseen Possibilities in Our Lives
by Molly Srode 6 x 9, 208 pp, b/w photos, Quality PB, ISBN 1-59473-050-42 **$14.99**;
HC, ISBN 1-893361-75-6 **$19.95**

The Geography of Faith: Underground Conversations on Religious, Political and Social Change   *by Daniel Berrigan and Robert Coles; Updated introduction and afterword by the authors* 6 x 9, 224 pp, Quality PB, ISBN 1-893361-40-3 **$16.95**

God Lives in Glass: Reflections of God for Adults through the Eyes of Children
by Robert J. Landy, PhD; Foreword by Sandy Eisenberg Sasso
7 x 6, 64 pp, HC, Full-color illus., ISBN 1-893361-30-6 **$12.95**

God Within: Our Spiritual Future—As Told by Today's New Adults   *Edited by Jon M. Sweeney and the Editors at SkyLight Paths* 6 x 9, 176 pp, Quality PB, ISBN 1-893361-15-2 **$14.95**

Jewish Spirituality: A Brief Introduction for Christians   *by Lawrence Kushner*
5½ x 8½, 112 pp, Quality PB, ISBN 1-58023-150-0 **$12.95** *(a Jewish Lights book)*

A Jewish Understanding of the New Testament
by Rabbi Samuel Sandmel; New preface by Rabbi David Sandmel
5½ x 8½, 384 pp, Quality PB, ISBN 1-59473-048-2 **$19.99**

Journeys of Simplicity: Traveling Light with Thomas Merton, Basho, Edward Abbey, Annie Dillard & Others   *by Philip Harnden* 5 x 7¼, 128 pp, HC, ISBN 1-893361-76-4 **$16.95**

Keeping Spiritual Balance As We Grow Older: More than 65 Creative Ways to Use Purpose, Prayer, and the Power of Spirit to Build a Meaningful Retirement
by Molly and Bernie Srode 8 x 8, 224 pp, Quality PB, ISBN 1-59473-042-3 **$16.99**

The Monks of Mount Athos: A Western Monk's Extraordinary Spiritual Journey on Eastern Holy Ground   *by M. Basil Pennington, ocso; Foreword by Archimandrite Dionysios*
6 x 9, 256 pp, 10+ b/w line drawings, Quality PB, ISBN 1-893361-78-0 **$18.95**

One God Clapping: The Spiritual Path of a Zen Rabbi   *by Alan Lew with Sherril Jaffe*
5½ x 8½, 336 pp, Quality PB, ISBN 1-58023-115-2 **$16.95** *(a Jewish Lights book)*

Spiritual Practice

Divining the Body
Reclaim the Holiness of Your Physical Self   *by Jan Phillips*
A practical and inspiring guidebook for connecting the body and soul in spiritual practice. Leads you into a milieu of reverence, mystery, and delight, helping you discover a redeemed sense of self.
8 x 8, 256 pp, Quality PB, ISBN 1-59473-080-6 **$16.99**

Finding Time for the Timeless
Spirituality in the Workweek   *by John McQuiston II*
Simple, refreshing stories that provide you with examples of how you can refocus and enrich your daily life using prayer or meditation, ritual, and other forms of spiritual practice.   5½ x 6½, 208 pp, HC, ISBN 1-59473-035-0 **$17.99**

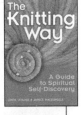

The Gospel of Thomas: A Guidebook for Spiritual Practice
by Ron Miller; Translations by Stevan Davies
An innovative guide to bring a new spiritual classic into daily life. Offers a way to translate the wisdom of the Gospel of Thomas into daily practice, manifesting in your life the same consciousness revealed in Jesus of Nazareth. Written for readers of all religious backgrounds, this guidebook will help you to apply Jesus's wisdom to your own life and to the world around you.
6 x 9, 160 pp, Quality PB, ISBN 1-59473-047-4 **$14.99**

The Knitting Way: A Guide to Spiritual Self-Discovery
by Linda Skolnik and Janice MacDaniels
Through sharing stories, hands-on explorations, and daily cultivation, Skolnik and MacDaniels help you see beyond the surface of a simple craft in order to discover ways in which nuances of knitting can apply to the larger scheme of life and spirituality. Includes original knitting patterns.
7 x 9, 240 pp, Quality PB, ISBN 1-59473-079-2 **$16.99**

Earth, Water, Fire, and Air: Essential Ways of Connecting to Spirit
by Cait Johnson   6 x 9, 224 pp, HC, ISBN 1-893361-65-9 **$19.95**

Forty Days to Begin a Spiritual Life
Today's Most Inspiring Teachers Help You on Your Way
Edited by Maura Shaw and the Editors at SkyLight Paths; Foreword by Dan Wakefield
7 x 9, 144 pp, Quality PB, ISBN 1-893361-48-9 **$16.95**

Labyrinths from the Outside In
Walking to Spiritual Insight—A Beginner's Guide
by Donna Schaper and Carole Ann Camp
6 x 9, 208 pp, b/w illus. and photographs, Quality PB, ISBN 1-893361-18-7 **$16.95**

Practicing the Sacred Art of Listening: A Guide to Enrich Your Relationships
and Kindle Your Spiritual Life—The Listening Center Workshop
by Kay Lindahl   8 x 8, 176 pp, Quality PB, ISBN 1-893361-85-3 **$16.95**

The Sacred Art of Bowing: Preparing to Practice
by Andi Young   5½ x 8½, 128 pp, b/w illus., Quality PB, ISBN 1-893361-82-9 **$14.95**

The Sacred Art of Chant: Preparing to Practice
by Ana Hernandez   5½ x 8½, 192 pp, Quality PB, ISBN 1-59473-036-9 **$15.99**

The Sacred Art of Fasting: Preparing to Practice
by Thomas Ryan, CSP   5½ x 8½, 192 pp, Quality PB, ISBN 1-59473-078-4 **$15.99**

The Sacred Art of Listening: Forty Reflections for Cultivating a Spiritual Practice
by Kay Lindahl; Illustrations by Amy Schnapper
8 x 8, 160 pp, Illus., Quality PB, ISBN 1-893361-44-6 **$16.99**

Sacred Speech: A Practical Guide for Keeping Spirit in Your Speech
by Rev. Donna Schaper   6 x 9, 176 pp, Quality PB, ISBN 1-59473-068-7 **$15.99**;
HC, ISBN 1-893361-74-8 **$21.95**

AVAILABLE FROM BETTER BOOKSTORES. TRY YOUR BOOKSTORE FIRST.

About SKYLIGHT PATHS Publishing

SkyLight Paths Publishing is creating a place where people of different spiritual traditions come together for challenge and inspiration, a place where we can help each other understand the mystery that lies at the heart of our existence.

Through spirituality, our religious beliefs are increasingly becoming a part of our lives—rather than *apart* from our lives. While many of us may be more interested than ever in spiritual growth, we may be less firmly planted in traditional religion. Yet, we do want to deepen our relationship to the sacred, to learn from our own as well as from other faith traditions, and to practice in new ways.

SkyLight Paths sees both believers and seekers as a community that increasingly transcends traditional boundaries of religion and denomination—people wanting to learn from each other, *walking together, finding the way.*

For your information and convenience, at the back of this book we have provided a list of other SkyLight Paths books you might find interesting and useful. They cover the following subjects:

Buddhism / Zen	Gnosticism	Mysticism
Catholicism	Hinduism /	Poetry
Children's Books	Vedanta	Prayer
Christianity	Inspiration	Religious Etiquette
Comparative	Islam / Sufism	Retirement
Religion	Judaism / Kabbalah /	Spiritual Biography
Current Events	Enneagram	Spiritual Direction
Earth-Based	Meditation	Spirituality
Spirituality	Midrash Fiction	Women's Interest
Global Spiritual	Monasticism	Worship
Perspectives		

Or phone, fax, mail or e-mail to: SKYLIGHT PATHS Publishing
Sunset Farm Offices, Route 4 • P.O. Box 237 • Woodstock, Vermont 05091
Tel: (802) 457-4000 • Fax: (802) 457-4004 • www.skylightpaths.com
Credit card orders: (800) 962-4544 (8:30AM–5:30PM ET Monday–Friday)
Generous discounts on quantity orders. SATISFACTION GUARANTEED. Prices subject to change.

For more information about each book, visit our website at www.skylightpaths.com